T0149210

RETURN TO *Nuna* LAKE

RETURN TO *Nuna* LAKE

HELEN HENDRICKS FRIESS

RETURN TO NUNA LAKE

This is a work of fiction. All of the characters, names, incidents, organizations, and dialogue in this novel are either the products of the author's imagination or are used fictitiously.

iUniverse books may be ordered through booksellers or by contacting:

iUniverse
1663 Liberty Drive
Bloomington, IN 47403
www.iuniverse.com
1-800-Authors (1-800-288-4677)

Because of the dynamic nature of the Internet, any web addresses or links contained in this book may have changed since publication and may no longer be valid. The views expressed in this work are solely those of the author and do not necessarily reflect the views of the publisher, and the publisher hereby disclaims any responsibility for them.

Any people depicted in stock imagery provided by Thinkstock are models, and such images are being used for illustrative purposes only.
Certain stock imagery © Thinkstock.

ISBN: 978-1-4917-9490-6 (sc)
ISBN: 978-1-4917-9489-0 (e)

Library of Congress Control Number: 2016906266

Print information available on the last page.

iUniverse rev. date: 04/25/2016

For Maureen

Chapter 1

Andrew Mellon woke in the morning to the sound of the rain hitting on his penthouse window. It wasn't the gentle splash of an early spring's rain. It was the harsh sound of the beating of the rain which was coming down quite hard. He walked to the door that led to his terrace and saw his plants bending in the wind. *I hope this doesn't keep up too long,* he thought. He had a new variety of a rose bush he was pampering. Even with the hard rain most of his garden was surviving the pounding storm. *Can things be famous*, he wondered. Well, his garden had been featured in some of the New York magazines. Not everyone who lives in a penthouse has a garden such as his. He had started with some greenery and rose bushes, but soon started to experiment and worked with specialists to develop them. He had to admit he enjoyed some of the fame it brought him, (being mentioned in a rose fancier's magazine). But this morning it brought him no real pleasure. Nothing seemed to bring him pleasure anymore.

He had been feeling so down and despondent the last few weeks. His home and his fortune gave him no good feelings. He felt very alone.

He heard a key in the lock and the cheery voice of Mima, his housekeeper.

"A cheery good morning, sir," Mima said as she shook the rain from her umbrella. "My dad would say it's only good for ducks, but I enjoy the way it cleans away the darkness and leaves things refreshed. I hope you had a good night's sleep. I'll get started on your breakfast."

"I just want coffee this morning."

"Nonsense. Your body is a machine that needs food. Would you like some pancakes?"

"I just want coffee this morning."

Mima looked at Andrew.

He could tell she knew he had another restless night. Seemed like he had a lot of those lately. *She's probably trying to figure out a way to get me out of this mood,* he thought. She had been working for him for many years: fixing him breakfast, cleaning his house, helping him with occasional parties. But he felt so down these days.

She spoke. "You are very good to me. Forgive me if I'm overstepping my place, but I can see a change in you lately. Is your health okay? Are you having business problems? Is there anything I can do to help?"

He looked at her quietly and asked, "How long have you been taking care of me, Mima?"

"Since Gretchen hired me."

"And you stayed with me through it all." He paused. "After all these years, I know nothing about you. Who are you really?"

"I was a woman who had no real skills seeking a job. Now I am a woman trying to take care of you."

He seemed deep in thought. "I'm afraid Gretchen was not very nice to you."

"No, she wasn't nice at all. But you were very nice and also very generous. I had a daughter who wanted to go to college." She paused and then continued. "I admit it. I knew Gretchen would not be around very long. You would need someone to look after your house and I wanted to be that person. And for me, it worked out very well. My daughter went into medicine and is now a doctor. You made that possible. I thank you for that. So does she. She wants me to quit working but I told her you still need me. One of these days you'll meet a nice woman who will take care of you. Then I'll quit."

"That will never happen, Mima."

"You're going to meet the right woman when you least expect it. Enough talk. I need to get you some food." Mima hurried into the kitchen.

There's no woman for me, Andrew thought. He admitted to himself that he was lonely. He had stock brokers to take care of his money; he had business managers taking care of his business, housekeepers to take care of his house, even a professional gardener to help him in the terrace garden he so enjoyed. But he had no one to share his life with. Someone to talk with at the end of a day. Someone to share his bed and every-day living with. Should he try to change his life? Part of him wanted to change; part of him wanted things to stay the way they were. He had a good life. He was satisfied with his life. Or was he?

He thought about his life with Gretchen. It had been short and sweet. It was she who had urged him to buy this penthouse even before they married, and then hired the top

3

designers in New York to decorate it for him. His home was featured in some of the top home magazines. But she was only in his life long enough to get things started. She met a wealthy Italian and in less than a year, left Andrew to move to Europe. *At least she didn't ask for money,* he thought. He and Gretchen were destined for failure.

Finally, to satisfy Mima, he did eat an omelet, some toast and coffee, and he had to admit he felt better. He thought about what Mima had said about the money she earned working for him. *Did it really make a difference in her daughter's life?* Money was just a commodity to him. Goodness knows, his grandparents were always pinching pennies.

He hadn't thought about his grandparents for quite a while. His father had died in Viet Nam before he was born and his mother died soon after. His grandparents had taken him in. They lived a frugal life, he thought, urging him to save, save, save. As he looked over their papers after their death he saw they had given it all to charity, not in a big lump sum, but giving it to help people through a crisis. He hadn't thought about money when he was growing up. In many ways he thought they were rich. They always had food on the table, their house was paid for; they seemed to have everything they needed or wanted. His grandfather was very proud of his Ford car and how long it lasted. Every Sunday afternoon his granddad would wash the car and polish it. He and his grandmother would admire it and then get in and they would drive around the countryside for an hour or so.

Andrew thought about his grandparents: how they took in when he was a baby, fed, clothed, and educated him. He never did properly thank them. That was wrong! He had thought them old-fashioned with their strict rules. He never lived with them after going away to college. *How ungrateful I have been. Did I ever properly thank them?*

He became aware that Mima had been chatting away. He had heard none of her stories. He felt ashamed.

"Mima, I'm afraid I haven't been a very good employer. After all these years I know nothing about you. Get a cup of coffee and sit and tell me about you," he told her.

"Well, I might just do that," she said with a smile. "I am one of the lucky people in life. I married the greatest man in the world who promised to take care of me forever. And he did. He died in an accident when our daughter was young." She paused and seemed deep in thought for a couple of minutes. "He left us financially set so that I could stay home instead of getting a job. That worked until I found out what college would cost. I looked for a job – one I could be home for my daughter after school. I heard about Gretchen looking for a housekeeper so I applied and she hired me. I remember the fight you two had over how much you would pay me. You insisted it had to be more than she thought I was worth. But you prevailed. All of that money went into my daughter's college fund."

"I didn't pay you those kinds of wages, I'm sure," Andrew said.

"Maybe not, but it was enough to start college and part-time jobs paid the rest."

"She must be very bright."

"She is. She's very successful now. Your generous gifts at Christmas helped us to succeed."

"I never knew any of this. Why didn't you tell me?"

"At first I thought Gretchen told you. I had told her about my reasons for working when I insisted on going home early or the time I didn't work because my daughter had some ailment. It was only when you were divorced that I realized that she was a liar and a thief." She sat up straight in her chair and said, "Sorry. I spoke out of order. I should not have said that."

"Forget it Mima. It took me a long time to realize that my life with her was nothing but a big lie. I've come to terms with it."

"Have you really?" Mima asked quietly. "I think you live a lonely life. You need a good woman to share your life."

"Mima, I'm settled in. I have women in my life when I need them. I have a life filled with many friends. And you know how busy I am all the time. I guess I don't have time for a woman."

"Uh huh," she said. "Maybe one of these days you'll wake up and see I'm right. Now, enough talking. I'm going to get busy."

Andrew listened to her sing as she worked. She had a pretty good voice, not bad at all. He continued to be restless. He looked around. Suddenly he realized how sterile his penthouse seemed. Everything was professionally decorated but there was nothing personal in the room. He looked at his dining room. He hadn't used it much. Gretchen left all those years ago. His marriage to her had been short. She spent a fortune of his money. But she hadn't asked for any money when she left. Her new husband had much more. Andrew had been wise (and lucky) in investment matters and had made a fortune in a short period of time thanks to the booming computer and internet business. After Gretchen left, he was even more into investing until it became his life. He realized he was a very wealthy man. He had many acquaintances, was in demand as "the extra man at dinner," respected by his peers. But he did not have a family, he realized as he sat in his big chair. *This chat I had with Mima is the most personal contact I have made for years. I don't have any real friends.* He sat there, quietly thinking about his life. He thought about something his grandpa told him. *A man is measured by the friends he has, not by his bank account.*

"Maybe you're right, Grandpa, maybe you're right."

Andrew paced the floor for a few minutes and found himself standing in front of the full length mirror in his bedroom. He took a really good look at himself. He was still as tall as he thought, just over six-foot, his hair was still the light-brown of his youth and had not yet started to turn gray. He was pretty lucky that way: his grandfather's hair had gone white when Grandpa was in his forties and Andrew was now nearing fifty. As he stood there taking a good look at himself, he decided he looked pretty old. He didn't work out much and it showed. He looked old and out-of-shape. He couldn't even remember when he had last been to the gym. He had always thought he looked, fit young and rather good-looking. But not today. He did not like what he saw.

He sat in a somewhat pensive mood as Mima tidied his home. He picked up the stack of magazines on his coffee table. The decorator had deemed them suitable for his lifestyle. He hadn't ever really looked at them. He supposed Mima brought them in and then threw them away. He saw he had several news magazines, a couple of professional magazines

7

for investors, a couple of others he couldn't identify. He saw a stack of magazines on the bookcase shelf that he recognized as old ones. *I wonder how much all of these magazines cost me. I have never read any of them.* He had also not thought about how much anything cost for many years. He picked up one of the glossy magazines from the shelf – *Classic Homes*. His fingers paged through the magazine until he saw a beautiful home on a high hill that overlooked a lake – Nuna Lake.

He read the article. It told of a woman who had purchased the home in Nuna Lake. It had been the main house of an estate many, many years before. Guest houses had been built for those who often came for a month or more, to fish, ride horses, play tennis, or simply to get out of the summer heat of the cities. The guest houses were gone now. No one had lived in the main house for years. It had finally been sold to a woman named Rose who restored it. She found many old records. At one time the house was known for its many gardens. They had been created by an old Cherokee gardener who kept meticulous records. Rose had uncovered these records and with the help of a local landscaper, she restored the gardens. As Andrew looked at the pictures he felt a strange feeling come over him – a restful, serene sort of peace. The gardens were beautiful. There were gardens of many flowers of one color. Some had many colors of just one flower. And, of course, there was a rose garden for "Rose". There were gardens that were formal and some that had old-fashioned beauty. Andrew became aware that he was feeling very peaceful looking at these pictures. He suddenly felt an urge to see these gardens for himself. He wanted to see them, to touch them, to… well, that would be silly. Or would it?

He was well respected. He thought they would certainly let him look at the gardens. He would even make a contribution to one of their charities if they wanted it. But as he looked at the pictures, he realized they'd probably laugh at someone so artificial that they pay for everything. But wait a minute, he thought. *That's the kind of life I lead. I think money buys anything.* Somehow or other Nuna Lake didn't look like that kind of town. What could he do? He spent the rest of the day listening to the rain. That night he dreamed about his grandparents and a garden of flowers in front of the big front porch. He had a mental picture of his grandmother, wearing an old straw hat, on her knees pulling weeds; he saw his grandfather watering the flowers for her each evening. Andrew slept very well that night.

He felt very refreshed when he woke the next morning. He grabbed his robe and headed for the living room and the magazine he had looked at yesterday. He turned to the pages with the pictures of the gardens of Nuna Lake. As he looked at them he felt an even stronger urge to go see them. A little voice told him he was being silly. But a stronger voice told him he had no responsibility to or for anyone. He could do whatever he wanted to do. But how would he do it? He knew he could fly there and back home in one day. He used his plane very little. A pilot was always on standby. Somehow the picture of him doing so was disgusting. These people in the pictures looked like *real* people. *Maybe if I drive out there I'll fit in better. I have no ties to keep me in New York. Yes, I think I'll go to Nuna Lake.*

He heard the key in the lock as Mima came into the foyer.

"Good morning, Mima," he said in an almost pleasant voice.

"Well, good morning to you. You're up bright and early this morning."

"I'm thinking of taking a trip."

"Any where special?" she asked.

"Uhhhh, well, no." He suddenly felt he wanted no one to know his plans. He had been such a private person all his life he wasn't sure he'd know how to share his dreams with anyone. He had dreamed about it last night. He knew he had to go there.

"Well, there's a big world out there. Do you think you'll be going right away?"

"Yes, but I'll let you know my plans." As he said that he realized that Mima would probably be the only one who would even care to know. "Could you fix me some biscuits and sausage gravy this morning? My grandmother always fixed it on Sundays for Grandpa and me."

"I'll fix it right away," she said, happy to see him interested in anything.

Andrew began to plan for his trip to Nuna Lake. He was suddenly subdued by the thought of his car. He only had one car – a limousine – and somehow it seemed ridiculous to be chauffeured on a vacation. It was equally silly to think about driving a limo to Nuna Lake. It was the only car he had. He needed a new car – one he could drive himself. He thought about it. He wanted to be one of the people in the picture, not someone who stands out in the crowd. He wondered what kinds of cars the people in Nuna Lake drive. He realized he didn't even know what kinds of cars people in New York City drive.

The more he thought about his car the more he realized he wanted no one to know who he was or where he was from. He realized he might not even be able to drive any more. It had been a long time since he had tried. Cars have changed. Maybe he forgot how to drive. He was glad he kept his driver's license renewed. If he bought a car the dealers might recognize his name. His name was well-known in investment circles. This would not be easy for him. Maybe he shouldn't try it. It had been too long since he lived the way most people do. Most people go to work every day. Could he hold down a real job? A job that let him get his hands dirty. He might be able to get a job in the business world, but there he would meet other business people. He had no skills to get a job with manual labor involved. If he even got a manual job what name could he use? He'd have to produce a Social Security card. Maybe people in small towns wouldn't recognize his name. He continued to pace the floor as he pondered his ideas. He was always very methodical with plans for his investments. Maybe he needs to be methodical about some plan about how to change his life. Or would it be better to just wing it? He could confess all if he is caught. Or maybe no one would care if a poor, forsaken man has the same name as some investor in New York.

Andrew paced the floor as he made a plan and then changed his mind. He realized he had not used real money for a long time. Some one always did it for him. How had he let his life get so out of control that he did nothing? Nothing.

I am not even a contributing member of society, he thought. *No,* he thought, *I am going to change my life.*

He went to his desk to get a pen and pad of paper. He began to write of list of things he would need to do: get a car, get license plates, etc. Did he need insurance? Well, maybe it's required. He was used to having people do these things for him. He would need some clothes. *I wonder how they dress in Nuna Lake.* He looked again at the picture. Most people were in jeans and casual tops. He had nothing like that. His clothes were all business-like and very formal. Of course he had his clothes for tennis and golf, but that was not the kind of clothes he saw. And he didn't want to show up wearing new clothes. What could he do?

He decided to eat his sausage gravy and biscuits in the kitchen so he could chat with Mima.

"Have you thought anything more about your trip?" she asked. "Do you have somewhere special in mind?" she asked.

"I'm thinking I might just get in my car and drive a while. Do you have a car?"

"I don't but my daughter has an old Ford car."

"If she's a doctor she must be able to get a newer car than that."

"She needed a car to get back and forth to school. Cars aren't important to her. Now she takes the subway to get to her clinic. She is trying to sell her car."

"Does it run good or need any work on it?"

"It seems to be fine, just pretty old."

"Could I see it?

"You must be joking. Are you doing this to be nice to my daughter?"

"Not at all. I might even want to restore it," he said. *Now that sounds like a reason for me to buy the car,* he thought, feeling rather smug to have thought of it. "I'd like to see the car."

"My daughter will be home today. Would you like for her to bring it here?"

"Mima, take me to your home to see it."

"Shall I send for your car?" she asked.

"No, Mima. You ride the bus to get here. Let's take the bus."

Mima was shocked. "Sir, I don't think your friends would approve."

"What friends, Mima? Anyhow, you know I always do what I want. Come on, leave the dishes. I may want to buy your daughter's car."

"But, sir..." she began.

'Come on, Mima, we'll have an adventure."

Reluctantly, she left the penthouse with him.

As they walked to the bus stop, he realized that it was the first time in years he had walked the streets of New York. He breathed in the fresh air and started to laugh at some of the sights he saw: a woman dressed in practically nothing trying to put a move on an old man; a mother with three small children; people buying magazines at a news stand. When they arrived at the bus stop he was suddenly aware he had no money for bus fare.

"Mima, I'm most embarrassed. I seem to have no money with me right now."

"Not a problem. I've got it."

Well, that's something else I'll have to learn: to carry money in my wallet. He was so used to have everything taken care of for him he had forgotten how to take care of himself. *I guess that's lesson number one: keep some cash in my pocket.*

The bus ride took him through parts of New York City he didn't know existed. It was exciting to him to see New York this way. They soon arrived in her neighborhood. It looked very pleasant: small neat homes with green grass and flowers in pots on people's porches. As they left the bus stop, they passed children playing on the streets who called out to Mima.

"You're a popular lady around here," he said. "Have you lived here long?"

"My husband brought me here as a bride. It's always been home."

He saw the old Ford as they approached the house.

"That's a beauty," he said as he saw the old Escort. He walked over to the car in the driveway.

"I'll get the keys," she said and returned almost immediately. "Why don't you look at the car, drive it around if you want to. I'll make some coffee."

He was almost afraid as he got behind the wheel. It had been so many years since he had driven a car. But he remembered enough. He drove it carefully around the block, began to enjoy driving so went around the block again and again. Then he returned and looked inside the hood. The joy of driving his own car came back to him.

Mima called to him. "Come and sit on the swing while we have coffee."

"Mima, I like the car. Would your daughter sell it to me?"

"Sir, what are you going to do with an old car in New York?"

"Maybe I'll restore it when I get back from my trip."

"I guess she would sell you the car."

"When will she be home?"

"Any minute now. She worked the night shift at the hospital and had to stay over a bit. She starts a new job next week. Here she comes now."

A dog came bounding out of the house and ran to meet her. The woman coming up the walk was beautiful: long dark hair, stunning figure, a bit of weariness in her eyes, but a big smile on her face. She put out her hand and said, "Hello, I'm Lauren. You must be Andrew, I mean Mr. ...."

"Call me Andrew. Yes, I am. Your mother told me you might sell me your car."

"What in the world would you do with this old car?"

"I'm not sure. I might restore it. I need a new hobby."

"Well, it might be good for that. I've had it for ten years and always kept it up to date on maintenance so it works well. But there's some rust on it and the tires need replaced and..."

"What price are you asking for the car?" he asked.

"I think the Blue Book prices it around $2000."

"Would you accept $3000 if I take it today?"

"I couldn't take that much for this old car."

"Trust me, I've got the money." Andrew started to feel he had to have that car. He needed it to get to Nuna Lake. No one there would suspect him of having money if he arrived in town in a very old car.

"Make it $2000. My mother taught me to be honest."

"Your mother is not a business-minded person. It's worth $3000 to me. Can we do the paperwork today?"

"Don't you want to have it checked out or something? I don't want to cheat you."

"I have plans for this car. It's perfect."

He pulled his cell phone from his pocket and called his business manager. "I'm on my way to the Secretary of State's office to buy an old car. Make arrangements for me to be able to have the title transferred to me so I can claim ownership today."

He put his phone back in his pocket and asked Lauren to get the car title. They left immediately. That afternoon he proudly claimed ownership of his 2003 Fort Escort.

"You probably should have asked $5,000 for the car," he told Lauren.

She laughed. "I told you my mother taught me to be honest."

Andrew felt he was on a cloud. It was the first step toward his new life. "Mima, take the rest of the day off. See you tomorrow," he told them as he proudly drove down the street in his 2003 Ford Escort.

He drove to the garage where his limo was parked. "Thinking about restoring it," he told the attendants who had gathered around, surprised to see him in such an old car.

With a smile on his face, he thought, *I have completed step one. Now I need some decent clothes.* He noticed a Salvation Army truck on the street as he walked home from the garage.

"Where do you take these things you pick up," he asked the driver.

He found the center was just a few blocks away. *Isn't it funny,* he thought, *how everything falls right into place when it's supposed to happen.* He slept very well that night, dreaming about beautiful roses. Maybe there would even be a place in Rose's garden for the new bush he was working on to develop: the color and the characteristics of the rose were unique. It was so beautiful, yet special in its own way.

The sun was shining brightly the next morning when Andrew woke. For the first time in more than a year he was excited and looking forward to his day.

"I hope you're not going to change your mind about the car," Mima told him. "I think you were much too generous yesterday."

"Mima, I have plans for that car. I have plans for myself. I told you I was thinking about taking a trip. I have decided to leave today. I don't know how long I'll be gone, maybe a month or more. You will continue to receive your paychecks as usual. You don't need to come to the house every day; but if I'm gone more than a month, would you please check things to make sure every thing is okay here. I'll call you when I return. Take the rest of the day off."

"Where are you going?" she asked. "Are you sure you're all right?"

"I'm going to follow my dream," he said quietly. She left, somewhat reluctantly.

He got out the oldest pair of slacks he owned along with a golf shirt and headed for the Salvation Army re-sale shop. Fortunately, the doorman was busy and didn't see him leave the building. What he saw at the shop surprised him. There was a section for absolutely everything: furniture, clothes, furnishings, well, just everything neatly arranged, ready for resale. He headed for the Men's Clothing section. His eye caught a bin of *gently used* clothes. He headed that way. Some of the things in this section were only twenty-five cents. *Are there really people out there who can only afford a quarter for a pair of jeans,* he wondered. He continued his search. The clothes were clean but well-worn. They were perfect. He chose two pairs of jeans, three knit tops, and a worn jean jacket. Then he headed for the shoe department. This was not so easy. He was a man with a big foot. He had his shoes specially made for him. He chose a pair of work shoes that he felt he could use. They weren't too comfortable but he decided they would have to do. *Maybe I should have some pain on my face to make me look authentic*, he thought. They put the clothes in a plastic bag that said *Salvation Army* on it. Once home he got his computer and mapped out his route. Then he gathered his razor and a few personal items, along with a favorite old jacket left over from his youth, and put them in the bag with the clothes. He was ready. He had never traveled so light before. He decided he would not change into his old clothes until the next day so no one would see him. Now he was ready. He headed for the parking garage.

"Good afternoon, Mr. Mellon."

"Hello, Jack," he answered.

"I'm sorry you had to walk. I could have brought your car to your place."

"I'm here for the old Ford," Andrew told him.

"Of course," Jack said. "Which restoration shop are you going to use?"

"I might check out a couple."

"Good idea."

He saw an ATM machine in the lobby.

"Haven't used one of these in a long time," he said. He really didn't know how to use one.

"You put your card in and take out your cash. It's pretty easy."

Andrew looked in his wallet and found a card with his bank's name on it. He put it in the slot and followed the directions. He was glad he had used his grandmother's birthday for an ID number. He was also very glad he had remembered the number he had chosen. He took out $500, the limit for one day. As he did so he thought it was so little. The thought occurred to him that $500 was a lot of money to most people. He tucked $300 into a secret pocket in his wallet. *I must make this $200 last for a while.*

Fortunately, he remembered to look at the gas gauge. He had a full tank.

Andrew got in his car and sat there. *Could he really do this? Could he really change his life?* He carefully started the engine. *This car is the greatest car in the world,* he thought. He was off to a new life. Someday, maybe very soon, he will want his old life back. But today he felt like the richest man in the world. He began his way out of the garage, out of the city. He was on his way to Nuna Lake. He was surprised at the freedom he felt for the first time in his life.

Chapter 2

Andrew sat up straight and tense as he started down the streets of New York City. It had been years since he had driven any car so he was very careful, trying to learn about his car as well as trying to remember the rules of the road. It didn't take him long to reach an expressway which led him to an Interstate. By this time he could relax a bit and start to enjoy his trip. He was surprised to see the way everyone seemed to be driving with authority. Well, he decided, he would drive that way too. He was able to relax a bit as he headed toward eastern Pennsylvania. When he stopped for gas he learned he had to pump his own gas. *When did that change,* he wondered?

Soon he was able to relax even more and began to look at the scenery. He turned on the car radio. Then he began to feel hungry. He decided to stop for lunch only to realize the time. It was nearly four o'clock. Where had the morning gone? Time to make new plans! He suddenly realized his route would take him within thirty miles of the town where he grew up. He decided he needed to see the town. He knew the farm had been sold to a housing developer and he would not know a soul, but he felt a compulsion to go there; to see the old town and to pay respects to his grandparents. He would stop for the night, get up in the morning and visit his old hometown. That sounded good to him. As he pulled into a motel for the night, he realized he really was making a change in his life. He felt good.

The next morning it took Andrew a few minutes to realize where he was and think about this new adventure he was on. He saw a young family having breakfast: a mom, dad, a son, two little girls, and a baby. The children were sitting up eating their cereal and the mom and dad seemed happy. They seemed to be playing a game of sorts with each other. Andrew had never thought about kids – his or anyone else's. But something about this family touched him. He loved the way they laughed together. For the first time, maybe ever, he wished he had a family. He headed for his car and western Pennsylvania where he would leave the Interstate and head for his home town.

He had no GPS system in this car, but it almost seemed as if the car had a mind of its own. He headed for the little town of Sheridan. The roads were new to him, but when he reached the town, he had no trouble finding his way to the area where his grandparent's farm had been. Andrew had sold the property to a developer. He saw a village of streets where he had played. He saw small children playing games. He couldn't tell exactly where his grandparent's house had been until he saw 'the view'. His grandparents would sit on the porch each night to enjoy it. He missed his grandparents at that moment and wished he could have just one more visit with them. He drove to the local cemetery and visited their graves. Then he made his way to a bench where he could sit and look at the river that ran through the town. On that day, with the sun shinning brightly and the river sparkling, he realized what a special place this was for him to grow up. He sat on the bench, remembering times past, remembering his Grandpa and Grandma. He wished…well, he never doubted they loved him, but would they love what he had become? A loner with no real friends. He grew up in a community where no one locked their doors; friends were welcome in any home. He sat on the bench lost in his thoughts. He may have money in the bank, but did it make him happy? He sat, pondering his life, and then decided to move on. Nuna Lake people in the picture in the magazine looked pleasant. Maybe he could find happiness there.

As he traveled for the next couple of days he visited motels and fast food places he had only heard about in commercials. He purposely looked for places that would be clean but unpretentious. He was a different man today than the man he was last week. He was seeing the world in a new light: one where people lived on fixed incomes; watched what they spent, yet seemed to have a happy life. He hoped he might find that kind of life when he got to Nuna Lake. Would his former life come to haunt him? How long did he expect to stay when he finally reached Nuna Lake? Would the people there see right through him? He began to be anxious. Finally, he saw a sign that said the town was only twenty miles ahead, then ten, and then… Nuna Lake.

While the sight of the town name excited him, he began to panic for a moment. A little voice inside of him said *you did this. This is what you wanted.* But an even stronger voice said *it's time for the next step in your journey.* He looked for a place to eat. There seemed to be a few places he could choose from: fast food, small cafes, etc. He finally chose the one nearest to him and went inside. It was a charming little café. There were about ten tables and everyone eating there seemed to all be sitting in one section. Andrew chose a table where he could sit and observe the people. Everyone seemed to know everyone else, yet there was no running back and forth among tables. Everyone seemed respectful to the others. He felt a little uneasy in his worn clothes and for a moment he wished he were a little more dressed up. But he did notice the men and women both had on jeans. This must be the expected way to dress in this town. He was approached by a waitress.

"Hello, I'm Kristi. You must be visiting Nuna Lake. I know everyone in town. Would you like a cup of coffee or maybe a cold drink to start with?" she asked with a smile.

"Yes, I just arrived in town. Coffee sounds great."

"Welcome to Nuna Lake." She hurried off to get his coffee.

She brought him coffee and took his order for the daily special.

"Tell me, is there a motel in town where I can stay for a few days?"

"Not in Nuna Lake – though we do have a Bed and Breakfast here. The nearest motels are out on the highway about three miles away. It's on the road to Sprucedale. None are very fancy but they're clean and have good beds."

After a delicious lunch with really fresh vegetables, Andrew left the diner, very content at that moment. He felt like he was meant to be here. He wanted to drive by the house to see the gardens but it was getting dark so decided to wait until the next day. He checked into the motel and found there was a small counter with a microwave oven and a small refrigerator in his room. *This is perfect, just perfect,* he thought. *Tomorrow will be my big day. I will get to see the gardens. But it will be the first day I really have to be a new person. Andrew Mellon lives in New York, is very rich and very lonely. Andy Mellon is a drifter who wants friends.*

Andy drifted into a hard, sound sleep. The next morning when he awoke he realized it was nearly ten o'clock. He hadn't slept this late for years. He lay there, wondering...wondering if it had been a bad decision to travel to Nuna Lake. He had a good life, people who took care of his every need, people who did his bidding. Here he was, in a small town where he had never been; he didn't know a soul, had a junky old car, no decent clothes... what was he thinking when he took off from his big city life? After a hot shower and clean clothes (he had worn the same jeans each day he traveled) and a cup of coffee made in the microwave, he began to smile. He was having an adventure. He hadn't ventured this far from his penthouse in years. He had made a start for a new life when he left New York. He may decide to go back there today or tomorrow, or whenever. Who would know, anyhow? But today he was going to have an adventure. He was Andy Mellon – a man without a job, $300 in his wallet, in a town he doesn't know. And he had the security of knowing that he could switch back to his old life any time he wanted. At that moment, he knew how lucky he was. He had no ties to anyone; he could walk away from Nuna Lake any time he wanted, send for his plane, and resume his old life. But at that moment he knew his old life was not what he wanted. He envied the families he saw in the restaurant, laughing together, having fun. But would he have the courage to see this through?

After this many days he was ready for one of Mimi's good breakfast. But instead he opted for the free breakfast in the motel. He had to be thrifty. He began to talk to the woman who was keeping the food containers full.

"You must be new to the area," she said as she poured him coffee. "Are you visiting Nuna Lake?"

"Yes, just here for a few days," he told her.

"You'll stay longer or you'll come back. Nuna Lake is a wonderful place to live."

"The town is certainly beautiful with all the flowers around."

"This town owes Mike Nelson a lot. He runs a landscaping place. It's out on Highway 16. He makes sure the flowers you see along the street are watered, deadheaded and the bushes trimmed. Nuna Lake wouldn't be the same without Mike."

"I heard about a big house he did something with..."

"You must be talking about Rose's house. It's so beautiful. You must see it before you leave town. It's been in magazines and everything. Rose made Nuna Lake popular. When Mike restored the grounds for Rose he put Nuna Lake on the map."

"Can I see it if I drive by?" he asked.

"Oh, yes. It's so beautiful. But you don't have to drive by. Rose and Mike don't care if people stop to look at it. Lots of brides want to go there for pictures. Rose and Mike make everyone welcome."

"Is Mike the same Mike who runs the landscaping business?" he asked.

"Yes. He's here at the motel now checking the plants in the lobby. Rose had hired Mike to restore her property. They fell in love and got married. This town loves Mike and Rose."

"They sound like special people."

"They really are special. Oh, look, here comes Mike now. Mike, Mike," she called to him. "Come and meet a newcomer to our town."

"Hello. I'm Mike Nelson," he said, offering his hand.

Andy rose from his chair. "Andy Mellon," Andy said as they shook hands. "You've become quite a famous man."

"Famous to just a few people, I'm sure," Mike offered as they shook hands. "Are you in town on business or pleasure?"

Andy was thrilled to be meeting the man who created such beauty. "I guess a little bit of business and a lot of pleasure." Then Andy surprised himself by adding, "I'm very pleased to meet you. Are you doing any hiring at your landscaping business?"

"We can always use good men and women. What's your background?"

Andy felt his heart go to his knees. What could he say?

"I have a lot of love and respect for our environment and the role of trees and natural elements to keep them healthy."

"You gave the right answer. Will you be in town long? Stop out at our plant and look us over. You may have ideas we can use to improve things."

"I'm flabbergasted," Andy told him. "You would listen to me?"

"It takes everyone to help make us great. I have to run now, but if you can, stop out this afternoon. I'll show you around."

Andy couldn't believe he had really met the great Mike Nelson. He wished he had his computer so he could find out more about him. Then he thought that maybe there was a library in town. They should have public computers there. As he paid his bill he asked the cashier for directions to the library. Once there, he spent the next hour learning about this special man. Mike had gone to school at Stanford, came home and opened his own business. Along the way he was selected by the EPA to do special testing for them. The list of contributions he had made for the environment was long.

Andy left the library and decided to drive around Nuna Lake. It was a beautiful, restful, little town. People were going in and out of various small shops. A few minutes later he discovered he was on a road that ran up and down hills along a beautiful, peaceful lake. It had to be Nuna Lake. There were many inlets along the way. He pulled in at several, got out of his car to simply look at the lake – so serene you felt like you had to stay a while. As the road made its way back to town he realized this was the road with the house and the beautiful gardens he had come to see. The view was magnificent. He had never felt such peace and serenity. He wanted to stop and just sit and take in the beauty but didn't think it would be wise to stop at this time. For a moment, while he was talking with Mike, he wanted to tell him about his work with the rose bushes he was developing. But he had to remember, he was not Andrew Mellon, the man from New York. He was Andy Mellon, an unemployed, but a new man out to see the world.

Chapter 3

As Mike Nelson drove away from the motel he thought of how lucky he was. After being alone for many years with a son to raise, he had met his Rose. Rose. The love of his life. He loved her more than he thought it was possible. He had to see her now. Then he had an idea. He had left the house early that morning and he was hungry. He saw a MacDonald's on the corner so stopped, got lunch for two and headed for home.

"Anybody here hungry for lunch," he called out as he went in the door. "Oh my, what smells so good?"

"I'm baking for the bake sale tomorrow. I'm taking six pies - two cherry, two apple, a pecan and a lemon cream."

"They smell wonderful. I brought lunch. Got time to take a walk and eat lunch on the bench?"

"What a wonderful idea. We haven't been out there for over a week." She put her mixing bowls in the sink.

The bench Mike referred to was a special, special place. When Rose had purchased the house she had inherited a garage full of "stuff": a canoe, an old desk, old tools, lawnmowers which had made her famous, and boxes, including one that contained records kept by the old Cherokee who had originally taken care of the house. The land had been Indian Territory; then purchased by a rich man from Chicago who had married a woman from the east coast. The wife could not adapt to the hot summers of the city and yearned to return home. The man wanted to make his wife happy so he searched for a piece of land where he could buy property and build her a summer home. When he saw Nuna Lake he knew it was a perfect place. He took great care when having the house built, including having everything transported across the lake and carried up the hill so as to preserve the land and the beautiful view from the site. The house was magnificent and the view was breathtaking. Then he built several summer guest cottages so guests could come and stay for a month or more. They had a beautiful young daughter. The old Cherokee had come to work for them to take care of the grounds. He loved this child and developed for her a beautiful secret garden in the woods. As the child matured she often entertained special young men there. The records showed this worried him. But he did nothing, perhaps because the records also showed *he* had feelings for the woman of the house. Rose was to later find writings in the house under some floor boards to show a love affair between the Cherokee and the woman of the house.

When Mike had found the old garden records in the box that had been stored, he decided to secretly try to find it. When he did find it, he quietly restored it. It was there that he first confessed his love for Rose, and she confessed her love for Mike. But they decided to keep their garden secret from anyone. And if anyone else ever discovered the place (and they did), each person seemed to realize it was a very private place that no one talked about. He placed a bench there beside a quiet pond at the bottom of a spring and planted water lilies there. He painted Rose's name on the bench.

It was to this place that Mike and Rose took their MacDonald's lunch; to quietly absorb the beauty of the quiet place that warm spring day.

"Met a new man today at the motel."

"What's his name and where's he from?"

"Andy Mellon is his name and I don't know where he's from. I had a strange feeling about him."

"A good or bad feeling?" Rose asked.

"I'm not sure. He seems like a drifter, but I'm not sure what he is. I think he's new to Nuna Lake. He asked if we were hiring. But his skin is pale, not sunburned like someone who has been working outside. There was an air of elegance about him: the way he talked and listened intently...I honestly don't know what to think about him. He asked me if we were doing any hiring and I told him to stop by the office this afternoon. Maybe I'll know more tonight.

They finished their lunch and then returned to the house.

Chapter 4

After lunch Andy paced the floor for half an hour and then thought the time had come. He got in his car and headed out for Route 16. He soon saw a sign that said *Mike Nelson Landscaping*. It was truly unpretentious. Andy expected to see some big sign or flashing lights or whatever. You could drive right by the place and never know it was there. But it was very, very big, covering probably a few acres. Andy saw groves of trees in one place, many kinds of landscaping stones and bricks in another. There was a huge greenhouse, a building where Andy saw what looked like a garage for lawn movers and other lawn equipment. He saw other buildings on the property. *Mike Nelson has quite a business here,* Andy realized. He saw a building with a small sign that said *Offices* so he headed that way.

As he opened the door he saw Mike talking with a receptionist. Mike put out his hand and said, "Welcome to my second home. This is Jenna, our receptionist. I was just telling her to expect you."

"Hello, Jenna," Andy said politely. Then turning to Mike he said "I hope I'm not coming at a bad time."

"There are no bad times around here," Jenna said with a smile. "Welcome to Nuna Lake."

"Let's go in the office and get acquainted."

Mike said. Andy saw an organized clutter of things. Books, magazines, brochures filled his desk. "One of these days this office is going to be neat as a pin," "But it will probably be the day my son, Tim, takes over my chair. Come and sit down. Tell me about you."

Andy was not prepared to talk about himself, but always the professional man he was, he decided to tell him the truth. Well, sort of the truth.

"I was in the business world for some years but had no home life. I'm trying to make a new start. I read about you in a magazine and decided this might be a place to start over. I admit I know little about landscaping but I'm willing to learn all I can, either by reading about it or with hands-on if you provide a teacher."

"Did you read about me in Classic Homes or some professional magazine?"

"It was Classic Homes. I found a copy one day. Nuna Lake looked like a good place for me to get a new start."

"Your departure from the business world, was it by request or for personal reasons?"

"It was strictly personal."

Andy could see Mike studying this man who sat across from him. *He's probably wondering if I am just out of jail — or maybe just out of a mental hospital. Would I pose a threat to Mike's staff?*

Mike sat quietly studying the man.

"What do you know about landscaping and lawn care?" he asked.

"Nothing. But I will work hard and have been told I learn quickly. I will do any work: sweep your floors, cut your grass. The magazine article I read was mostly about your wife, but there was enough in it about you to make me realize I would like to work for you. If you'll let me work for you for three days (in case I flub up the first two) you can send me on my way. You won't need to pay me."

Mike looked at the man who was speaking. "You owe me no explanations. You do have an air of mystery about you. But I like some mystery in my life. Let's give it a try."

"That sounds fair enough."

Just then the door to his office opened and a big man with red hair and a big smile came in.

"Oops, sorry. I didn't know anyone was in here. I'm Gabe," he said putting out his hand.

"Gabe, meet Andy Mellon. Andy is joining us and you will need to teach him everything," Mike said.

"That sounds like a big order," he said with a smile, shaking Andy's hand. "What kind of work do you know how to do?"

"I have been in the business world for a long time, but I used to cut grass for the neighbors and tend to their gardens."

"Well, we have a lot of that around here. Do you want to start work right now? I'll show you around the grounds."

"Are you sure I wouldn't be interrupting?"

"Are you through with him, Mike?"

"Let's let Jenna have a few minutes so he can get on the payroll."

Gabe took Andy to Jenna's desk to start the paperwork.

Gabe gave Andy a quick tour of the different sections of the plant. Andy saw a building with a small sign that said 'Research Lab and Design.'

"Mike works closely with the EPA. He's trying to develop a grass that won't require much water, yet still look green. He's also working on some different kinds of flowers and even working on a new rose."

Andy almost choked when he heard about the new rose. Oh, what he would give to see what was happening. He thought about his own rose bushes on his own terrace in New York. He had no doubt they were receiving good care. Marv, the professional gardener he had hired, came almost every day to check on his plants. Andy thought for a minute about whether or not he should end this scam. But there was something interesting about Nuna Lake. Everyone seemed so friendly and pleasant. He certainly had been treated well.

After the tour, Gabe brought Andy back to the office.

"You have a wonderful place here. I think maybe I'm out of my element but I do appreciate your letting me be here a while," Andy told Mike.

"You'll find Nuna Lake welcomes strangers," Mike said, and then he added, "I'm about to leave for home. If you have no plans for dinner, maybe you can join Rose and me. She's a great cook."

"I-I-I couldn't impose. But I really, really, really would enjoy seeing your gardens."

"Just follow me home. Everyone wants to see the gardens and Rose does enjoy showing them off."

This man could probably afford a limo but he's driving an old truck, Andy thought as he followed Mike home. But he also had another thought. *I'm going to finally see the beautiful gardens I read about.*

As Andy pulled into the driveway of Mike and Rose's beautiful home he was suddenly mesmerized by the beauty of the land. Everywhere you looked there were patches of color: sometimes mixed colors and plants, others were just a splash of one color with the flowers standing tall and regal. Andy was drawn to them as if being pulled. How could anything be as beautiful as this? As he stood by the flowers he was almost transfixed, unable to move.

"Hi, I'm Rose."

He turned to see a beautiful woman greeting him.

"I'm Andy and I'm in awe of all this beauty."

"Well, there is history on my side and a wonderful man who made it all come alive for me."

"It was a labor of love I assure you," Mike added. "Andy, meet Rose. Rose, this is Andy. He'll be out here one of these days, weeding it, cutting the grass, deadheading the flowers...."

"And I'll love every minute of it, "Andy added.

"You must have worked with a lot of flowers," she said.

"No, not really. I had a small garden for a time. I grew up on a small farm with my grandparents. My grandma always had the usual summer plants. Nothing as grand as this." He stood there shaking his head.

"It is special. Why don't I show you around while Mike starts to cook the steaks. I thought we'd eat out on the patio since it is such a warm night."

"That would be wonderful, but I never expected anything this special. It's so, so....."

Rose started to laugh. "Come now with me. This is my old fashioned garden with spring tulips and daffodils. When the tulips and daffodils are gone, I'll have cosmos, marigolds and other summer flowers. They are so beautiful."

They made their way through the various gardens. And then they came to the rose garden. Andy had never dreamed it would be so magnificent. There were roses of nearly every color getting ready to bloom. He looked at the tags; some of them were roses Andy had only read about. He felt like he had died and gone to heaven. He sighed deeply at the beauty of it all. At that moment he knew he had made the right move to come to Nuna Lake.

Mike called to them. "Steaks are almost cooked. How do you like your steak cooked, Andy?" Mike asked.

"A bit on the rare side if it's not too late."

"Just in time."

As they ate their dinner Andy began to feel, well, embarrassed or ashamed that he was not being honest with these people who were being so good to him. He laid his fork aside and sat looking at his plate.

"I hope your meal is okay," Rose said.

"You have made me most welcome. Much better than I deserve."

"You owe us no explanations," Mike said.

"Thank you for that. I want to assure you I am not a murderer, or rapist, or anyone on the run. I am a man seeking a new way of life. I have never been in so welcoming a town as Nuna Lake."

"Nuna Lake is wonderful," Rose said quietly. "When I came here I was still suffering from the effects of a broken marriage. I had very little desire to get on with my life. Nuna Lake welcomed me with open arms. No one asked questions. The trees and bushes on this property were so overgrown I could not even get into the driveway when I first saw this house. But I had a sense of peace while I was sitting on the front porch. It was Mike who saw the potential for this house when I hired him to cut the trees away from the driveway. This house has quite a history."

"I knew it was special when I saw the pictures in Classic Homes," Andy said. "But I don't think Classic Homes captured nearly enough of its beauty."

"I think it's time for pie," Mike said.

"And then I must head out," Andy said.

"Where are you staying?"

"At a motel on Route 16. But I'll be looking for a room. Are there rooms available in Nuna Lake," he asked.

"I don't know of any," Rose said.

"I guess I'll stay at the motel while I look around," Andy said. "But I must leave now. This day, this evening, has brought new meaning to my life. Thank you, thank you."

Chapter 5

Just before seven the next morning, Andy pulled into the parking lot at Mike Nelson Landscaping. He was surprised to see so many people already starting work. Trucks were being loaded with mulch and other landscaping products, tools were being sharpened. As he made his way to the office, Gabe called to him.

"Good morning," he called. "I think you should start your day in the hospital."

Andy stopped and looked at the man. "I'm not sure I understand: in the hospital?"

Gabe started to laugh. "Yep, come this way."

Andy followed, very puzzled, and then he started to laugh. It was a hospital for plants.

"Let me introduce you to Martha. She's bossy and sassy and about to be fired and…"

"Hi, I'm Martha," she said holding out her hand.

"I'm Andy," he said.

"Hi Andy. Just ignore the smart aleck remarks from the side lines. Welcome to my home away from home. We not only take care of sick plants but we do tracking on all sorts of research products. We make an entry each day about any changes in them. It takes time but is a wonderful research tool." She stood looking at him. "I see Mr. Wise Guy did not give you a shirt. Let me grab one for you. I guess you'll need an extra large." She reached onto a pile of green T-shirts with the name "Mike Nelson's Landscaping" on them. "Just put your shirt in the locker room. It will be safe there. Tonight just throw this shirt in the container there. The night watchman will wash and dry them tonight so they'll be clean tomorrow. Here's a baseball cap for you to wear. Mike wants us all to look alike."

Gabe spoke. "I'm leaving you in good hands, Andy. See you later."

"Come this way and I'll show you the kinds of things we look for here," Martha said. Andy quickly changed his shirt and followed her into a room that looked sterile.

"Wow! I can't believe this. Who would ever think so much research would be taking place?"

Martha just smiled. "Each plant has its own notebook. We keep very good records here. You won't be assigned to record the information until you are well acquainted with the plants. But you need to learn about them. Over in that section is the grass Mike is trying to develop for the EPA. Only three people go into that section: Mike, Gabe, and me. Over here we have…."

Andy followed her, completely surprised to see the amount of research going on in a small town. Mike must really be respected in the field, he thought.

Finally, at last she came to a section and told him it was were he would be working that day. He would be repotting plants that had grown too big for the pots they were in. He would inspect another section of plants to look for bad bugs. Another section had seedlings starting to grow. Andy could scarcely take in the many different things happening here. And this was just one building on the property. *Mike Nelson must be a highly respected man in the business.*

"I want you to transplant these seedlings into small pots today. This is the way you will do it." She proceeded to do one with such speed that Andy wondered if he missed something. She certainly knew her business well. She left him alone to begin his work.

Through the big greenhouse windows he could see a flurry of activity taking place on the grounds. It appeared that everyone was working hard, yet there seemed to be a friendly atmosphere in the air. People were smiling and friendly. Gabe came by and told him a food truck would be by at 11:30 with lunch. Everyone would work and leave between 4:30 and 5:00 p.m. He left Andy alone.

Martha came by when the food truck arrived and told him he was doing a good job. Andy was not sure he would pass her inspection. He loved what he was doing: getting his hands in the soil, feeling it in his fingers. He realized that he had done very little with the new rose bush he wanted to take credit for developing. The work had been done by a man he paid. Yet he took credit for its success. He felt a bit like a phony but then thought maybe he had earned at least a bit of credit. He had studied the plan and had made many suggestions after studying about the different varieties of roses. And he had funded the project. But that was such a small part of the process. *I guess I owe a lot of other people for my successes. But now I am in the real world. I see how hard it has been for people along the way.* But he wondered...*how much of his success did he owe these other people?*

At the end of the day he threw his T-shirt in the laundry and made his way to his car. He was very tired. When had he ever done so much in one day? Then he thought about how much physical labor was involved for those working around him: the men cutting grass, digging out plantings, working on the equipment. He was not out in the hot weather with the sun beating down on him. He was not doing any physical labor so many were doing. When had he ever thought about all those who worked around him, keeping him comfortable in his New York penthouse...well, he decided, he had made a good choice to see how the rest of the world lives.

As he left the premises that evening along with many others, he saw an old car pull up as people came out of the plant. Almost immediately two young children jumped out of the car, crying out "Daddy, I'm here." They ran to embrace him. The man lovingly reached out to pick up the youngest toddler and touched the other child. He leaned in the car and gave his wife a kiss and got in to be driven home. At that moment Andy envied that man more than anyone in the world. *He has it all. As long as he makes enough money to feed, clothe and house his family, he is a rich man.*

At the end of his third day, Mike came to him.

"Well, I did give you three days, as you requested. Do you want to try for another three?"

"If you'll hire me. I would like to stay. It's been a long time, if ever, that I have done any physical labor, maybe working on the farm when I was a boy, but I feel very content. I would like to stay on if you'll hire me."

"Martha was impressed about your eye for detail at your work. She would like to keep you with her, but I think we'll save those jobs for rainy days and send you out with the road crews tomorrow. Are you up for that?"

"I'll try any job you give me."

Three weeks passed. Andy had moved from job to job and found he could do most anything he was asked to do. He learned how to dig a hole to plant a tree or bush. He learned that cutting the grass meant more than pushing a mower. It also meant edging, trimming, and cleaning up all the clippings. He learned about different plant food – how much and how often to use. He learned why different plants need different environments. He loved every minute of it. He was making friends with a lot of different people. They were all friendly, nice people.

One night when he was leaving work, Mike walked out with him.

"Have you found a room yet?"

"Not yet. I've been looking in the newspaper. I wasn't sure if I'd have a job."

"Why don't you follow me and we'll go see Harry. He's a man who lives alone. His wife died a couple of years ago. His three children live out of town. They worry about him being alone. He's capable of living alone, but they worry he might fall and no one would be there. He has a big house. For many years he ran the only hardware store in town, but eventually the big dealers bought him out. He's a great guy. I talked with him the other day and told him about you looking for a place. I don't know if he's ready to have someone live with him. But I think you two should meet."

As they approached Harry's home, Andy saw a big house with a beautiful view of Nuna Lake. Harry came out to greet them.

"Hello, young man," Harry said as he greeted Andy with his hand outstretched. "I hear you are looking for a room."

"I believe I am. I didn't get fired from my job yet so I can pay the rent."

"Rent, sment," Harry said with a smile. "I snore very loud, but I'm down the hall from the room you'll have. This is a new idea for me and I'm not sure it will work, but I'm willing to give it a try. At least it will get my kids off my back. They think I'm too old to live alone, but I won't go and live with them. I love my home. Millie and I loved this house." Harry seemed a little loss in his memories for a minute. No one said anything.

"What are you going to charge to come take care of me?" Harry asked.

"I don't believe you understand, sir. I will be paying you for a place to call my home for a while," Andy said politely. "I believe your family knows you are well able to take care of yourself. I'm new to town and don't especially like living in a motel. There aren't too many nice rooms to rent on a short term basis. I'm new at my job and may not be able to do the work. Staying with you for a week or so would give me a chance to find out if I can do it."

"What did you do before you came to Nuna Lake?" Harry asked.

"I was in the business world in New York. I was born and brought up on a small farm. I needed a change in my life. I read about Nuna Lake, came here, and Mike gave me a job. If he fires me tomorrow, I'll have to move on. I'll pay you any amount you want to charge. I don't drink or smoke, or carouse around with women," he said with a smile. "I'd like to give life in Nuna Lake a try. I will leave any time you think best."

"I wish Millie was here to tell me what to do," Harry said softly. "Millie was my wife. She died. We were married almost seventy years. She could judge people better than anyone I know. I really miss her."

The three men stood quietly together as Harry mourned for his beloved wife.

Then he raised his head and said, "Millie never allowed me to weep and mourn. She always said life was too short. We have to move on. Maybe I have to move on, too." He thought quietly for a minute. "What do you like to eat?"

"I'll take my meals in town. I just need a place to sleep."

"I'll give this arrangement a try. Do you want to stay tonight?"

"Maybe Andy should see the room first," Mike suggested.

"That won't be necessary," Andy said.

"Go get your things and come on back. We might as well give this a try," Harry said.

Andy looked at Mike who nodded his head.

"I'll get my things and be back in an hour."

"Don't stop to eat. I made soup today. Maybe you'll share some with me. I'm not a very good cook but I try."

Andy could see a small smile come onto Mike's face.

"I would love a bowl of your homemade soup. I'll get my things and be back in an hour."

Chapter 6

The next couple of weeks passed quickly. Andy couldn't believe how his life had changed. He was a different person these days. He actually enjoyed getting up in the morning and going to work. He looked forward to how he would spend his day. Whoever thought he'd enjoy this kind of life. Things were working out okay with Harry. Andy knew Harry thought of Andy as a babysitter (and wasn't happy with it) but they respected each other. Now they almost liked each other. Harry told Andy the history of Nuna Lake and introduced him (through talking) to almost everyone who lived there. Harry cooked dinner every night and invited Andy to share it so he didn't have to eat alone. Andy found he looked forward to going "home" after work.

One night Tom, a man he worked with, told him some of the men were going to a local ballgame and invited Andy to go with them. He became friends with Tom, Tom's wife, Judy, and their children, Hobie and Katie. Andy worried he might be taking advantage of their friendship but he couldn't think of any way to repay these people who were making such a difference in his life. They invited him into their family.

Sometimes he felt he was being dishonest not to tell them who he was, but he was afraid if he did their friendship would change. He wanted it to last at least a little bit longer.

Everyone kept talking about the Fourth of July and how they would spend the day. He asked Harry about it. Harry told him about the parade in town in the morning, picnic in the afternoon, and fireworks in the evening.

"Harry, how about you and I go together to celebrate?" Andy asked.

"You go with your friends."

"You are my friend."

Harry sat quietly. "Millie and I used to watch the fireworks from the front porch. She wasn't able to get out very often."

"Tell me about Millie. What did she look like? "What did she like to do?"

"She was the prettiest girl in town when I married her. And she was the kindest, sweetest, smartest person I ever knew. We were married when we both were quite young. I had a job clerking in my father's hardware store. But we shared our goals in life. When my father died, I took over the hardware store, we had kids, and you know the rest." He paused for a moment "I really appreciate the way you let me talk about the old days. I appreciate having you here. I didn't realize how lonely I had become. My kids are still after me to sell the house and move closer to them. I suppose the time is coming near when I will have to do it." Harry sat quietly with his memories. Andy said nothing.

Finally, Andy spoke. "At work they tell me about the picnic in town after the parade. It sounds like something we shouldn't miss. Why don't we plan to go together?"

"No, no. You must find a woman and go have a picnic with her."

"I was married once. It didn't work out. She married someone else."

"That was her loss. You are a good man, Andy Mellon."

Andy was taken aback with shock. What had he ever done for anyone? What would the people he was making friends with think if they knew who he really was? And the thought occurred to him that maybe he was taking a job someone with a family needed to do.

"I'm not as good as you think. I have made many mistakes in my past," he said quietly.

"And you came to Nuna Lake to get a new start. Many people do. Not everyone fits in so nicely, but you do. You have a lot of friends here already who don't want you to leave."

"I don't think I know that many people."

"You are well-liked and respected in town. You may not know their names but they know you and like you. I will go to the big picnic on the holiday with you. We'll go at lunch time. Everyone brings something to eat and we share it after the parade. You can even go swimming in the lake if you want. Everyone has a good time."

"Do you think I'll fit in?"

"We'll go together. We'll have to take something to eat that we can share." Harry sat quietly, thinking about what to take.

"Why not let me buy something?"

"We'll buy something together." They thought for a minute. "They have an ice cream truck that will be there. People contribute to it so everyone can have some. There's a jar on the counter in the diner that everyone throws in their change to pay for the ice cream. Let's contribute to that," Henry said.

"That's a great idea."

Andy paused a moment and said, "My grandparents always celebrated the holiday by hanging out a flag. You have a flag pole in your side yard. Let's put the flag up and really celebrate."

"I know right where it is. I haven't hung it out since my Millie died. It will be a little bit like having her with us. Thank you for thinking about it."

The big day arrived. Harry and Andy ran the flag up the pole; then Harry saluted and started to sing The Star Spangled Banner. Andy joined in. Together they made their way into town.

"You have a good voice, young man. You should join the Church Choir."

"I haven't been in church for a long time."

"We'll go on Sunday. Then we'll have dinner at the diner. Then we can sleep all afternoon."

The celebration on Independence Day was like nothing Andy had ever seen before. It was almost like he had been there all his life. His new friends waved and called to him. There were no strangers there. Most everyone brought something for a big buffet table. They ate the usual fried chicken, ham, hamburgers, hot dogs, meat loaf, all kinds of salads and vegetables, cakes, pies, and pastries of every kind. Then there were games: a softball game, organized games for the children with a prize of a quarter, boating and swimming on the lake. Everyone seemed to know everyone else. Toward evening the high school band started a concert. People sat on blankets on the lawn and at dusk they got ready to watch the fireworks that would take place.

Andy spread out the blanket they had brought. Tom, Judy, and the children came by.

"Okay if I put our blanket next to yours?" Judy asked.

"We have a big blanket. Come and share ours," Harry said

Little Katie snuggled next to Andy. He had never been around children and wasn't sure what to do. But he liked it! He reached out and snuggled her closer to him. They were near the outer rim of the area of people. The music was loud and stirring at first; then the band switched into some old standards so everyone could sing along. Andy didn't know when he had ever felt so content.

As they sat there enjoying the music, they were interrupted by a loud screeching of a car that was coming down from the road above them. It was speeding, not on the road, but through the grass, through the crowd, running over people who were sitting there. The car finally crashed into the ice cream truck that was down by the water. There was screaming, crying, and mass confusion. Those people who could, reached out for each other. The descent down the embankment took less than fifteen seconds.

Andy immediately grabbed Katie to see if she was all right. Then he looked for Tom, Judy and Hobie. What he saw shocked him! Tom and Hobie had been run over by the car and were lying unconscious on the ground. Judy, who was stunned and bleeding, was trying to get to her feet. She reached for her husband and child. For a second Andy just stood there.

Judy was trying to wake up her husband and son. She had massive cuts on her face and body. The blood streamed from the wounds.

Moving from her husband to her son she cried out, "Tom, Tom, wake up! Wake up, wake up, Hobie" she called to him. "Wake up." She was trying to shake them into consciousness.

"I'm a medic, let me through," a voice called, and a man knelt beside them. He reached Tom. "Someone start CPR" he called.

"I'm a nurse," a woman called as she came running to kneel down beside Tom.

The medic looked at Hobie and gasped.

Young Hobie's body was a mass of protruding bones. He was alive but unconscious. He was breathing very shallow breaths. There would be no way to start CPR if he stopped breathing. There did not seem to be any part of his body that was not injured.

The nurse and others who came to help tried to resuscitate Tom, but soon it was clear that he was dead. His mangled body showed no signs of life. Still they kept up with the procedure.

Some people hurried to the car that had caused the accident. Inside were two teen-age boys, both apparently dead.

Trained personnel arrived on the scene. They ended the CPR being performed on Tom. They took his body to an ambulance. They looked in horror at Hobie and wondered how to move him to a stretcher for transport to a hospital. How could they even lift this small body onto a stretcher?

Judy, bleeding badly from her many wounds, knelt by her son. She continually told him to wake up.

In all the chaos, Harry had reached out for little Katie and said "Come with me, little one. Let's get away from this chaos. I'll keep you safe." He led her away from the scene and to her aunt who was nearby.

The fire department had a truck with medics on the scene almost immediately. There were bodies everywhere. Some who were mobile were taken by individual cars to the hospital in Sprucedale.

It was easy to see that Tom and his son had taken the brunt of the full force of the car as it careened down over them. And nearly took Judy also.

Someone gently took Judy aside so the medics could help her son.

Tom had died instantly on the scene. The medics turned their attention to Hobie. He had many broken bones, most sticking out of his body. He still was not conscious. Judy stood there. She continued to scream for them to wake up. Her anguished cries could be heard for miles.

Andy went to Judy and pulled her away from the scene and to the ambulance that would transport her son. Then he went back to the scene. He could see Tom was dead but at least Hobie was still alive. He was being carefully loaded into an ambulance.

Andy started for his car to follow the ambulance when Harry approached him. "Tell Judy that Katie is safe and is with Judy's sister."

Would the hospital in Sprucedale be able to handle injuries of this kind? Andy had never seen anything like this. It was like looking into the soul of someone.

Harry walked with Andy.

"Katie is going home with her aunt," Harry called. "I have a ride home. Go to the hospital. Your friends need you."

Andy hurried to his car and followed the ambulances to the hospital. He again thought about Hobie. He will need major, major help. Andy knew the man to help him if he was to be saved: David Hass: a man who specialized in children's surgery after college and med school. A man who was now one of the top orthopedic surgeons in the country. A man Andy had roomed with in college. Andy had been in his wedding and David attended Andy when Andy married Gretchen. Andy reached for his cell phone and called his old friend who practiced in Chicago.

"There's been a disaster in Nuna Lake. A car went out of control, killed at least three and injured many others. There's a young boy....bones sticking out all over his body. Can you come to Nuna Lake immediately?" he asked after identifying himself. "I'll have a plane bring you here. This boy will die without your help."

"I can't go barging into a hospital and demand to see a patient," David said.

"But he's breathing and alive. The nearest hospital is in Sprucedale, a pretty small one, and a small medical staff. This young boy needs you. It's too late to help his father. You're the only one who can save him He's a young boy...his bones are sticking out everywhere," he kept repeating. "You're the only one who can save him. I'll pay you any amount. Please, please help him."

"Maybe they won't let me help him."

"They'll let you. Money talks. I'll build them a whole new wing for the hospital."

Things were quiet for a moment. Then very quietly David said, "Send your plane. Maybe they won't let me see him but I'll try. Have the plane at the airport in forty-five minutes. I'll go there right now. See you soon."

After a couple of calls to make sure a plane would be ready Andy went to the emergency room to try to find Judy.

The doctors were working on Hobie. He heard one of them say he had never seen so mangled a body. But they ignored those injuries as they tried to stabilize his physical condition.

Judy would not leave Hobie's side despite her own injuries. She saw Andy standing there and thought of her other child.

"Where's Katie, where's Katie," she began to scream.

Andy went to her. "Harry took her away from the scene. She's safe. Now she's with your sister."

She barely heard him. "Tom's dead. Tom's dead." Andy put his arms around her and tried to calm her. Then she began to scream again. "Where's Hobie? Where's Hobie? Is he dead too?"

"The doctors are working on Hobie."

"I have to see him. I have to see him," she screamed.

A nurse came by, heard her screams and said, "I'll let you look into the room but we must stay out here to let the doctors help him."

She opened the door slightly so Judy could look into the room. It was impossible for her to see Hobie as he was surrounded by doctors, nurses, technicians, equipment etc. Then the nurse gently said. "Let me take a look at the cuts on you."

"No, no. Where's my husband?" she cried. "Where's my daughter?"

Andy went to her. "Your sister is taking good care of Katie. I'll bring her to you, if you need to see her."

"I want my husband," she cried. "He's dead. I know he's gone." She wept bitterly.

He put his arms around her and held her tight as she wept. Finally, she became calmer and then she started to sob quietly. Andy held her and let her cry. The night soon passed. Toward dawn the tears stopped. She finally went with the nurse to have her wounds attended.

The doctor finally came out of the emergency room to talk to Judy.

"We have stabilized Hobie's condition."

"Will he live?"

"His pulse is strong."

"Can I see him?"

"Of course. Come this way. We will keep him in this room so we can monitor him. His pulse is steady. That's a good sign," the nurse said.

Judy leaned over the body of her son. She spoke to him. "You have to get well. You're the man of the house now. Daddy's gone." She held his hand and began to weep quietly. "Don't leave me, don't leave me," she kept saying.

Judy's friends began to arrive to comfort her.

Andy made his way from the scene.

Even though he knew he was probably early Andy headed for the local airport. His friend David would soon arrive. But he didn't want to waste a minute. He drank some coffee and watched the sun come up. Soon he saw the small jet arrive with his friend. He was so anxious for David to be involved.

"Andy, Andy, it's good to see you." David said as he got off the plane. "You know the hospital may not let me see the boy. Is he still alive?"

"Yes, he's alive; just barely."

"How did you happen to be here when the accident happened?"

"It's a long story I'll tell you later. But there is something you need to know." Andy paused, and then swallowed hard. He had to reveal his identity, at least to this man. "People in this town know me as Andy Mellon, a drifter in town who works at a landscaping place. I cut grass and do all the usual things. No one knows me as Andrew Mellon of New York City. I hoped no one would ever know, but this boy's life is too important for secrets. His father died in this horrid accident. It's not the time to tell people who I am. But this boy must have the proper help now or he may be handicapped the rest of his life. I hope you'll keep my secret."

David sat quietly for a minute. "Do you have a story made up about how I happened to be on the scene so quickly?"

"I guess I don't."

They sat quietly for a minute. Then David spoke, "If I need an excuse I guess I could tell them I was fishing in the area and heard about the trouble and I wondered if they needed help. If they say they don't, then I have to go home immediately. Deal?"

"That's fair enough. These are good people in this town. They will want this boy to have the best. Here we are at the hospital."

Andy parked his car and they went in the Emergency Room doors. It was still filled with people needing help. David went immediately to the receptionist.

"Is your chief of staff here at the hospital?"

"Yes, he's in the OR. Please leave your name and I'll ask him to call you."

"I must see him now. I'm a doctor. Perhaps I can help. Will you at least tell him I'm here to help out if I can." He handed her his business card to give the doctor.

She hurried into the treatment room and came back immediately.

"Dr. Nelson will be out in a minute."

"Frank Nelson," the man said as he came out extending his hand toward David.

"David Haas," Dave answered. "I was fishing in the area and heard of the accident. I'm really an orthopedic surgeon, but can help anywhere you need me."

"Dr. Hass, everyone has heard of you. We have wounded everywhere – some seriously injured; some I think our medics can help. We must have more than fifty people injured. And we have at least three people dead. We do need more help. I've read in the journals of the miracles you perform. I would so appreciate your help."

"Let me get into some scrubs. Is there a room nearby to change?"

"Barbara," Dr. Nelson said to a passing nurse. "This is Dr. Hass. He's going to assist us. Show him where he can change and put him to work. I have to get back in the ER." He turned to David. "We are in the process of stabilizing a young boy.

He's been gravely injured. Would you look at him to see if you can help him?"

"I'll go right in."

It was dawn before the doctors and nurses could stop their frantic efforts. But their energy paid off. There were no more casualties that night.

Chapter 7

Andy returned to the waiting area outside the room where Hobie was being treated. He looked around the waiting room and saw Judy surrounded by her family and friends. She still was sobbing, uncontrollably at times. She could not believe her beloved Tom was gone. Andy sat down in a chair near the door. He felt compelled to be there, yet he wondered if he was intruding in Judy's space. He sat with his head in his hands. He looked up and saw Mike and Rose Nelson come into the room. They went immediately to Judy, reached out to place their arms around her and comforted her as best they could. Then Mike saw Andy sitting alone.

Mike came over to Andy.

"We started to watch the fireworks from our front porch last night and thought they had just ended early. We thought we heard sirens but we went to bed. Imagine our surprise when we turned on the radio this morning and heard what happened. Were you at the picnic?"

"Yes, Harry and I went together. We had a wonderful day. Then we spread out a blanket to watch the fireworks. Tom, Judy and the kids came to sit with us. We were having a very nice time until....I guess you heard about the car careening down from the road to the water."

"Yes, I heard. And now those two young men are dead."

"Harry took Tom and Judy's daughter to Judy's sister. Judy's still in a state of shock, I think," Andy said.

"I guess Hobie's pretty bad."

"It's terrible, just terrible."

"I understand some famous doctor was in the area and came to help," Mike said.

"So I hear," Andy muttered. He saw Rose approaching them.

"I want to take Judy home and put her to bed for a least a few minutes," she said.

"How is she?" Mike asked.

"Terrible. She's lost her husband and may lose her child." Rose paused. "She's refusing to go because she doesn't want Hobie to be alone."

"Maybe I can convince her to go home for a while. I'll stay here with Hobie," Andy answered. He got up and walked toward Judy.

"Judy, it's been a long hard night for you. You have been strong through it all. Let me help you. I'll camp outside the room where they have Hobie. I won't leave for a minute. You go home, check on your daughter and try to rest for an hour. I'll call you if there is any change. You must try to at least lie down for a few minutes. I promise you, I won't leave this room and I'll call you if there is any change."

Rose spoke, "Judy, let me take you home. You can at least take a shower and change clothes."

Judy looked down at her blood-stained clothes. It was the first she had noticed them.

"I guess I do need to change clothes." She looked at Andy. "Promise me you'll call me the minute Hobie wakes up."

"I promise you I won't leave his side," Andy answered.

"Do you think Hobie will make it?" Mike asked.

"When I saw him I didn't think so. But a specialist, Dr. David Hass, was in the area. He's from Children's Hospital in Chicago. He heard about the accident and came to help. He works miracles."

"I heard someone famous had arrived to help."

Mike and Andy sat quietly for a few minutes.

Mike then quietly said, "I really appreciate the way you have been with Judy through all this. She still has so much to go through. This might not be the time or place to say this, but when the time is right, will you please tell Judy I will continue to keep Tom on the payroll through the end of the year. It may help her not to have to think about money. And you don't have to worry about money either. You will continue to receive your weekly check. Please continue to support Judy any way you can. Let me know if she needs anything, from moral support to money. Anything. You needn't return to work until this crisis is over. I know Judy needs help now. She trusts you. I hope you'll be there for her."

Andy was stunned into silence by Mike's words. "How can you do this for me? I'm a stranger in this town."

"You're not a stranger any more. You are part of the Nuna Lake Family."

Just then David Hass came out of the Emergency Room. He saw Andy talking with someone. He walked to Andy and said, "Didn't I see you with the mother of the young boy in there?"

"Yes. Is he going to make it? Can you help him?"

"And who are you?" Dr. Hass asked Mike.

"Mike Nelson. Thank you for being here to help. Can you help the young lad?"

"The boy's dad and I both worked for Mike," Andy said.

Andy could see David almost smile at the thought of Andy Mellon working for this man. But very smoothly he concealed his amusement and said, "We finally got the boy stabilized. He is critically injured and may need many surgeries if he is to walk again. I would like to explain things to his mother. Is she still here?"

Mike spoke, "My wife took her home to rest but she can bring her back in twenty minutes. I'll call her now." He reached for his phone and moved a few steps away.

"Andy, I hope I won't blow your cover. I don't know what is going on and I don't have time to listen to it right now, but I bet you have a heck of a story to tell." He spoke quietly to Andy and then went back to his patient.

Some twenty minutes later, Judy and Rose came rushing into the waiting room. She had changed out of her blood-stained clothes but still looked very weary. "I'm here now. Can I see my child? Is he still alive?"

David came out of the room then and went to Judy and introduced himself.

"I'm Dr. David Hass. I work out of Children's Hospital in Chicago. Your son is alive now. His condition is very critical. He has multiple injuries. We have now stabilized his condition but he is a very sick lad. The next twenty-four hours are critical. Let me take you to see him."

Judy stood by her son's side. She tried to reach out to touch him but found she could only touch the many bandages on his body.

"Stay strong, son, stay strong," she keep telling him.

The doctor then led her out of the room so they could talk.

"He will need extensive surgery. I specialize in this type of surgery and will do the surgery but I need to move him to Chicago to do it. You have a good hospital here but it is not equipped to do the type of surgery he needs. We now have him in a stable condition. If we have no changes for twenty-four hours, I want to move him to Chicago. We have a fully equipped operating room there that is set up to handle problems of this sort. Please don't think about the money. We have many benefactors who will gladly pay all the expenses." He said this very sternly with a slight roll of the eyes in Andy's direction. "If you agree to this decision and if he survives the next twenty-four hours, I'll arrange his transfer to our hospital. I know this comes as a shock to you but we really don't have much time to waste."

Judy, Andy, Rose and Mike stood listening to Dr. Hass.

"Doctor, I would appreciate your doing whatever is necessary to save his life," Judy said quietly.

"We'll put him in a medically induced coma so he'll feel no pain as we move him. I will arrange for a medical ambulance plane to transport him. We'll do another full assessment of him and schedule surgery as soon as possible. I make you no guarantees that this will go well. But I have done this surgery many times before."

Mike spoke up. "Thank you, sir, for being here and taking on this patient. You won't need to find a benefactor to cover the cost. In Nuna Lake, we take care of our own. We want him to have the best, and that appears to be you. You make the arrangements and send the bill to me. Already the people in this town are collecting money to help bury our three victims. We'll get the money it costs."

"I have to return to Chicago now for I have a consultation scheduled for today and I have surgery scheduled tomorrow morning. I will order the ambulance plane right now. They will let me know when you arrive there." He turned to Judy. "There is a Ronald MacDonald house on the campus where you can stay. You do know, I hope, that this is a long road for your son. We may have multiple surgeries, slow healing, and some set-backs. But we will do all we can to return him home – a happy, healthy boy."

After he said these words, he looked at Andy and said, "I wonder if I can bother you for a ride to the airport in half an hour or so."

"Of course. I'll be ready when you are," Andy said.

As David and Andy pulled out of the hospital parking lot to go to the local airport, Andy asked him, "Do you think you can save his life?"

"I'm going to try. I think we can. But we never know for sure," he said quietly. "I really feel bad for his mom. She has had no time to think about the loss of her husband. Is she a strong woman?"

"I really don't know her too well. I work, I mean worked with her husband. He was such a nice man. It's hard to think he is dead now."

"Andy, are you ready to talk about how you got to this place? I admit I was surprised to hear from you."

"I really don't know how to tell you," Andy said quietly. "One day I woke up and realized I had a penthouse but I didn't have a home. I had things but I didn't have a family. I don't think I had missed them at that point. I stopped going to work some years ago when I found people wanted me to talk more about how to make even more money than to do a job. My marriage was over. I led a lonely life. I decided I wanted more. I wanted to get dirty doing a job and go home and collapse on the bed. I bought an old car, bought some old clothes and ended up in Nuna Lake. This is a wonderful place to live. The people are kind and caring. I got a job with Mike Nelson. He is an unofficial leader of the town. He keeps his eye on everyone. But I am living a sort of secret life. I'm not sure anyone in town would know who Andrew Mellon, the money man from New York, is. But I don't think it would matter to them. I am accepted for who I am. And I have loved every minute of it. Except, of course, I do have some qualms about not being honest with these good people. At first I thought I'd only be here a week or so and move on, but I've been here a couple of months already. I don't think anyone in New York even misses me. But I do have money in the bank. And I want this boy to live. Even if it takes every cent I have, I can earn more. I want Hobie to be made whole."

Chapter 8

When Andy returned to the hospital, he saw Rose sitting with Judy who was trying to absorb the changes in her life. Andy knew she was now accepting that her beloved Tom was gone. She will never again feel his arms around her...they will never again share a laugh while they sit on the porch swing... they will never again... He knew she was also thinking about Hobie. Her eyes kept darting to the emergency room. How would she survive if she lost Hobie also?

Rose sat in a chair beside Judy. "Mike checked out Dr. Hass on the computer. He has a wonderful resume and reputation. I think he'll really be able to help Hobie."

"But Rose, what am I going to do? Travel to Chicago to be with my son or stay here to bury my husband? I have to make the final arrangements." Judy was distraught.

Rose sat quietly letting Judy face the terrible decisions she had to make: be a grieving wife or a mother; be in Nuna Lake or Chicago?

Andy went to her.

"Is the boy okay?" he asked Rose.

"There is no change. Judy is trying to decide whether or go with Hobie or stay here and bury Tom."

Andy had thought about her problem. He knew what he had to do. He knelt in front of her.

"Judy, when I came to Nuna Lake and went to work at Mike's, Tom was the first friend I made here. You both welcomed me into your home and made me feel like one of the family. I want to do something for Tom. Let me go to Chicago with Hobie. You stay here and bury your husband. You can come to Chicago after the memorial service. I'll call you every hour to update you on his condition. I'm sure they'll keep me informed."

"I can't ask you to do that. You need to work."

"Mike has already told me I should put you first. I will be happy to do it."

Rose spoke. "Why not accept Andy's offer? Hobie will not know the difference. Andy can keep you updated. When the service for Tom is over, you can go to Chicago."

Judy sat quietly thinking.

"Are you sure?" she asked Andy.

"I'm sure."

"Tom really liked you. Now I know why. I'll accept your offer."

Rose spoke quietly. "I think Tom would approve. Would you like me to go with you to make final arrangements for Tom?"

"Yes, I'd appreciate your help."

Judy turned to Andy. "Thank you for your kind offer. I think Tom would be pleased."

Judy and Rose left the hospital.

Andy sat there quietly for a moment, the events of the past hours catching up with him. It had been nearly thirty hours since he had slept. He had very little to eat during the time. He hadn't really thought about such things. He shut his eyes for a moment when he heard a voice speak to him

"I think you've been here long enough. Go home. Get some rest. You have a big day ahead of you tomorrow."

He looked up to see Gabe speaking to him.

"I guess I am tired. Did you hear I will not be at work for a while?"

"Yes, I heard. This is a wonderful thing you are doing for this family."

"Was anyone at work today?"

"Most everyone showed up. Mike pulled all of us to go to the lakefront. There were so many people trying to help as soon as the police were done, that we have completely restored the place. Everyone wanted to help in whatever way they could. We couldn't help the families involved in this terrible scene but it helped to be doing something. A scout troop policed the whole lakefront for papers, etc. and we did some new plantings. We'll never forget the horror of it all but at least we don't have to be reminded every time we look at it."

"Nuna Lake is quite a town," Andy said slowly.

"It's a great place to live. Go now, and get some rest. You have a big day ahead of you. I'll plan to stay the night until Judy or you come back in the morning."

"If you are sure…"

"Go."

Andy made his way from the hospital to his car, and finally he saw the lights on at "home". He really felt like it was home. He parked his car and made his way inside.

Harry came right to him.

"Are you okay now?" he asked. "Come and sit in the kitchen while I heat you up some soup. Then it's a hot shower and bed for you. Has there been any change in Hobie's condition?"

"No. They're moving him to Chicago in the morning. I'm going with him so Judy can stay here and bury her husband. Then she'll take over in Chicago. He's going to be there for a long time."

Harry served Andy some hot soup and crackers. After eating, Andy pushed the bowl aside and headed for the shower. When he went to his room he saw the bed had been freshly made with the covers turned back.

"Harry, I don't think I've ever been made so welcome anywhere. I can't believe you would do all this for me."

Harry said, "I have to make my bride happy. She was always doing for others while I did my thing at the hardware store. I guess you heard about the car."

"You mean the car that ran over them?"

"Yes. The brakes failed. The boys had pooled their money to buy the car. They were told the brakes were bad. But they couldn't resist taking it out on the holiday. Now they are both gone," Harry said quietly.

And now there were three families grieving.

As Andy huddled under the covers on the bed, he said, "Thank you, Harry. I didn't know people could be so kind."

"Sleep well, friend."

Andy slept deep and hard until he heard his alarm go off at the usual 6:15 a.m. He took another quick shower and then got things ready for his trip to Chicago. He was glad he had spent his first paychecks on getting some clothes. He had nice looking jeans, slacks, neat looking shirts and a pair of loafers. He thought he would look decent to travel. He went to the kitchen and found Harry there at the stove with scrambled eggs, bacon, and hot coffee ready.

"Harry, you should still be in bed."

"No, I should be and I am getting you ready for a mission. I hope Hobie survived the night."

"I think they would have called us if he had died," Andy said. "Thanks for doing this for me. I guess it's an example of Nuna Lake hospitality."

"I hope we are all good people," Harry said quietly. "Go with God, young man. See that young Hobie comes home as a healed little boy."

Andy looked at Harry and realized that Harry was grieving for his wife, friends, his town and....

Andy reached out and gave Harry a hug. "I'll keep you posted each day I'm there."

Judy was already at the hospital when Andy arrived. The hospital had provided a chair and Judy was sitting close to the bed of her son. Andy heard her talking to him He stood back for a couple of minutes to let her have time with him.

He saw the medics arrive to move him to a stretcher for his trip to Chicago. Andy went to Judy and gently drew her away so they could move him.

"Promise me that you'll keep me informed about everything," she pleaded.

"It will only be a day or so until you are with him. Were you able to get the arrangements completed for Tom's service?"

"Yes. The service for the two boys is a combined service and will be held this afternoon. Tom's service will be tomorrow."

"So much grief," Andy said shaking his head.

The nurse interrupted them telling him they had to do final preparations for Hobie's transport to Chicago. "I understand the plane is at the airport."

Judy gently bent over her son, telling him to be brave, telling him to be strong, and that she would see him soon. She told him she loved him.

Andy led Judy out of the room as she softly sobbed for her son.

Almost immediately, Mike and Rose came to Judy and led her away from the area. Mike came to Andy and said, "Remember, if Judy or you need anything, anything at all, please call us. Thank you for going with him."

It seemed to take longer to get Hobie settled in the plane than for the plane to travel to Chicago. Andy was surprised when they got there. The ambulance crew very professionally moved Hobie to the hospital. David Hass was waiting when they arrived and immediately took him into surgery. Andy felt a small sense of comfort that they had made it this far. He saw a sign that said "Chapel" with an arrow pointing down the hall. Andy made his way there. It was empty. He sat in the silence, praying that God would guide the surgeon's hands and that Hobie would be healed.

One hour passed slowly. Then another. At one point, someone came from the operating room to tell Andy that everything was going as expected. He called Judy. Finally, at last, he saw the bed bearing Hobie being moved to the recovery area. Andy saw David coming toward him.

"That's one mangled little body," David said while slumping into a chair.

"He's still alive?"

"Yes." He paused. "This first surgery was mainly in the heart area. There were bones pressing on the heart walls making it difficult for him to breath. We moved things around so it will be easier for him to breathe. It really was more difficult than I thought. I have never done this kind of surgery on so young a child. But we had no emergency take place. He is still alive. The next twenty-four hours will tell us if the strain was too much for his little body." David looked a bit weary. But his face was hopeful. "He's heavily sedated but you can go in and see him for five minutes every hour." David sat with his head in his hands. "I hope I've done enough to keep him alive."

Andy looked at this watch. He knew the service for Tom would probably be ending. He dialed Judy.

"Hello. This is Rose answering for Judy."

"Rose, this is Andy. Hobie is out of surgery."

"Andy, Judy collapsed right after the service. I don't think she can talk on the phone yet."

"Is she okay?"

"I think so. We're in the process of getting her to bed. Her folks are here to take care of her. But there's no way she can come to Chicago today. Could you possibly stay for another couple of days?"

"Of course. I'll stay as long as needed. Let me tell you about Hobie so you can tell her."

He proceeded to tell her what the doctor had said. "If there is any change I'll call right away."

Andy had begun to think about how much money all this would take. He heard about Nuna Lake taking care of its own. He had contributed to the jars that sat on the counters at the stores and businesses, but he knew that the town probably had no idea of the real cost. He knew what he needed to do. He made his way to the offices to talk to business manager.

"I come to you today to ask you for help," Andy told the woman. "Nuna Lake is a small proud community. There are contribution jars on the counters of the stores to collect funds to pay this child's bill. The people are giving as much as they can, but I'm afraid they have no real idea how much this all costs. How can I contribute a large amount without anyone knowing about it? I still want them to be billed so that they will have the knowledge that they helped."

"What kind of money are you talking about?"

"What kind of money does it take? A new piece of equipment, a new wing? Here is the phone number you can call to verify who I am. I have the funds. Dr. Hass can also verify that I have the funds.

"Are you aware that Dr. Hass has indicated that there are to be no charges for his service? Perhaps the town's funds will cover the rest. His father had a very comprehensive insurance policy. Let me get some figures together and then talk to my superiors. I will be happy to work with you.

"Here is the phone number of my business manager who should receive the billings. You can check him out. But one thing, I want as few people as possible to know about this. I can't take away the pride of the whole town. They want Hobie to be healed."

Andy went back out and sat in a chair and waited for a chance to see Hobie. There was a coffee station outside the door of the waiting room. He decided to get some coffee, or maybe he should head for the lunch room. He stepped into the hallway.

"Andrew Mellon, is it really you?"

He heard a voice calling his name. He looked in that direction.

"Lauren." It was Mima's daughter calling to him. That same Lauren from whom he had bought his car. The same Mima who was always so good to him.

"What are you doing in Chicago?" They both spoke at the same time.

"Me, first." Andy said with a smile. "How did you get here to Chicago? I thought you were in New York."

"And I didn't know where you were. My mother will be greatly relieved to know you're okay."

"I've never been better. Is Mima okay? Are you okay?"

"We're both fine. Mom thought you'd only be gone a couple of weeks. When you didn't return she got anxious." Then suddenly Lauren, aware of her surroundings, said, "Are you really okay? What are you doing at Children's Hospital?"

"My story will take some time to tell. But I'm here because the son of a friend of mine was critically injured in an accident and he was brought here for surgery."

"Would it possibly be Hobie?"

"Yes, but how did you know about this child."

"Word travels fast in the medical circles. We heard in New York about the terrible accident. I may specialize in Children's Orthopedic Medicine. The hospital sent me here to observe Dr. Hass perform his surgery. He is a genius. What that man can do...." She shook her head back and forth.

"I'm here with that child. It's a long story. I'm here because the mother of the child is burying her husband this afternoon. I'm filling in for her until she can get here."

"But I know that they brought him here by ambulance plane. Where are you living?"

"It's a long story. One I've tried to keep secret."

"Can I at least tell my mother I've seen you? She's worried about you. We only expected you'd be gone a short while, no longer than a month."

"Do you have time to talk? Do you have to stay here? Could we have a late lunch or dinner? I've not eaten since breakfast. They tell me there is a very nice restaurant on the other side of the parking lot. Let's go there. I think they'll let me carry a beeper in case there is a change in his condition. I haven't eaten since morning and I'm famished. Let's go."

Together they walked to the restaurant.

"I'll tell you anything you want to know about me but first tell me about Mima. Is she really okay? She's the one person I thought maybe I should tell about my plans, but I didn't want her to worry about me. So I decided to say nothing."

"She's worried about you ever since Gretchen left all those years ago. She'll be so happy to know you are alive and well, and I must say, looking happier and healthier than ever."

"I miss her. She has been my only friend for all these years."

"She would be pleased to hear that."

After they were seated and placed their order, Lauren said, "Now start talking and don't leave anything out. My mother will want to know everything."

"Well, I was a pretty sad case, I now realize. I didn't need to do anything because I had enough money to pay someone else to do it for me. After months of feeling sorry for myself I picked up a magazine. Inside was a story about a place called Nuna Lake. I suddenly had an urge to go there. I wanted a new *way* of life; I wanted a new life. But I wanted no one to know who I was or where I was from. I bought your old car (which I'm still using), some old clothes and headed for Nuna Lake. I decided to stay there. I got a job working for a landscape developer. I work forty hours a week, getting dirty, getting tired. I told no one who I was. Hobie's father became my new friend. He was killed in the accident that injured Hobie. I was with Hobie's parents and little sister when the accident occurred. When I saw how badly Hobie was injured, I knew of only one man who could save him: David Hass. David and I were roommates in college. He came as soon as I called. I told David about my secret life and I found he did value our friendship. He came immediately. I told him to send me all the bills. I asked him to please keep my secret of my past life. He is honoring my request. But it turned out that Nuna Lake takes care of its own, and fund raisers started in town. Since his father is gone, my boss said to help out the family as much as possible."

"Wow, that's quite a story. And no one questioned you about your past?"

"No, I'm told that's the Nuna Lake way. There is no prying in someone else's affairs. I'm Andy Mellon, someone who drifted into town looking for a place to stay for a couple of weeks. And I feel I could stay forever. I still drive your old car: it works well. If anyone suspects I'm someone else, they are keeping it quiet. I go to work everyday, cut grass, plant flowers, or do what I am told. But tell me about Mima. Is she okay? Does she need anything?"

"Your generous paychecks go into the bank each week. She thinks you might need it someday."

"She's the one person who I thought would understand. She was always so good to me. Well, I guess I was a lonely old man. But I feel so alive, so vital, so needed these days. A few may suspect, but no one in Nuna Lake really knows what a fake I am."

"You're not a fake. You were a man seeking a change in his life and it would appear you have found it."

Just then Andy's beeper from the hospital lit up. "This means Hobie's is waking up. I need to get back to the hospital. Are you in town long?"

"No, I fly back on the midnight plane. I have to present all the new techniques I observed to a group of doctors tomorrow. I learned a lot watching Dr. Hass."

"Lauren, this has been a very pleasant surprise. Give my best to your mother. She is a very special lady."

Andy hurried to Hobie's bedside. For the first time since the accident, Hobie looked as if he were sleeping. Andy reached out to hold Hobie's hand. He looked down on this little boy who had been through so much.

"Is he sleeping or still under medication?" he asked the nurse.

"Both. But his vital signs are good considering what he's gone through. He'll probably sleep for a few hours. Feel free to go to your room and get some rest. We'll take good care of him."

"His mother had to bury Hobie's father today. I must call her now. I know she'll probably be here tomorrow. I'll be staying until she gets here."

"Then let me bring you a pillow. That chair opens into a single bed of sorts. Maybe you can get some rest there. Can I bring you coffee?"

"No, I'm fine. You've been very kind."

"All of us around here are really encouraged by how well he's doing. He's a strong little boy. No one would recognize this child as the one who was brought in earlier. We're all praying he makes it."

Andy reached for his phone to call Judy with the good news. She began to cry uncontrollably. Then Andy heard a voice on the line.

"This is Judy's mother. What did you tell my daughter?"

"That Hobie is through the surgery and is sleeping peacefully. The surgery probably saved his life. I'll stay by his side until she gets here. I imagine he'll be sleeping most of tomorrow so if she needs more time..."

Judy's mother interrupted. "I know she'll be there tomorrow. Thank you for staying with Hobie."

Early the next morning the nurse entered the room and began to talk to Hobie. "Wake up you sweet young thing. It's a beautiful day and you're on your way to recovery. Your mother is going to be so happy to get that news."

She looked over at Andy and said, "Oops, I should have talked quietly. Sorry."

Andy said, "It's not a problem. Is Hobie really doing well?"

"His vital signs are good. He was pretty heavily sedated but I expect him to wake up this morning."

"I'll call his mother right away." He dialed her cell phone.

"Good news," he told her when she answered.

"My sister and I are on our way to Chicago right now. I'll be there in an hour or so," she told him. "Thank you for being with him and for calling me. I'm stronger now. I know I have to be for my kids. Why don't you head for home?"

"I'll wait till you get here. I know he'll be glad to see you."

Andy looked over at Hobie. "Wake up, Hobie. Wake up. Your mom is going to be here soon and you need to smile at her. Wake up, Hobie."

Chapter 9

As Andy drove home and got closer to Nuna Lake, he realized how anxious he was to be going home. *Home.* He couldn't remember the last time he had ever felt that way. It had been years since he thought of using that word. Yet he was anxious to get there. He hoped Harry was okay. He was a bit concerned because he thought Harry sounded depressed. Could it be just about the horrid accident and Hobie's injuries? Maybe he's thinking about his wife. Her picture was in every room of the house. When Harry talked about her he got a special look on his face. Andy had to admit it. He liked living with Harry. He liked having a friend. He decided to phone him and tell him he was on his way.

"I've missed you. I'm glad you're coming home. I have some news for you," Harry said.

Andy decided to drive a little faster. *Maybe I should take Harry out for a late lunch*, he thought. Soon he was in Nuna Lake. People on the street recognized his car and waved to him as he made his way into town. He honked his horn and waved back. *Was he becoming one of THEM — a Nuna Laker?* He was heading home.

"I really, really, missed you when you were gone," Harry told him. "But I have some news for you. I have decided to go see my daughter, Angela. I'm not planning to move there, just visit for a week or so. Being by myself again these last few days made me realize how much we all need others in our life. I had become like a hermit living here before you came. You brought new joy to me. Now I feel I can go, have a nice visit, and come home. I have just one worry. After being away for a while do you still want to live here? Have I become a responsibility or a burden you feel responsible for?"

"Not in the least. I guess that means you'll let me live here while you're gone."

"Of course. I want you to feel like this is your home. At least until you find a pretty young thing and get married."

"I tried it once," Andy told Harry. "It didn't work out very well."

"Don't be afraid to try again. You're a good man, Andy Mellon."

And a liar, Andy thought. *I wonder if I could tell Harry about my past. Would he understand or be upset?*

"Thanks for that big delicious lunch. I didn't get much sleep in the chair last night. I think I'll take a nap."

Early the next morning he phoned Judy and found Hobie had slept well and appeared to be waking up. He told Judy to plan to go home for the weekend to be with Katie. He would return to Chicago to stay with Hobie. He decided to go to work to share the good news. Work at Mike's almost came to a stop as everyone crowded around him to get the latest news on Hobie. *This is a place where people care about each other,* he thought.

After work that night Andy got to thinking about Hobie. He wanted to take a present to him when he returned to Chicago. He decided to ask Harry for advice about a gift.

"You'll have to ask Sarah about that," Harry told him. "I'm just an old man who doesn't know much about kids. Sarah has a gift shop on Main Street and always knows the best thing to buy."

The next day after work Andy headed to Sarah's Card and Gift Shop. It was the first time he had really done any shopping and wasn't sure he'd find anything appropriate there. But at least he'd try.

"Hello, you're Andy and I'm Sarah. Welcome to my shop." He was greeted by a beautiful young woman with her hand held out in greeting.

"Hello, Sarah. Thank you for your warm welcome. I'm a man on a mission. Harry told me you have all the answers."

"Harry is a dear. We all love Harry. We're glad you're staying with him. I know he gets so lonely for his Millie. You must be looking for something special."

"I don't know if you've heard, but I've been spending time....."

She interrupted him. "You must be thinking about a gift for Hobie."

"How did you know?"

"Everyone in town knows how you went to be with Hobie. It was a wonderful gesture on your part. And now you want to buy him a special gift. Am I right?"

"How did you know, or is the Nuna Lake underground working again?" He looked around the shop. "Looks like you have a wonderful shop here. But do you have anything suitable for Hobie?"

"Well, let's look," she said. "Here's a beautiful figurine of a young boy with a baseball bat. And here's one with a mother, father, sister, and older brother. It could rest very nicely on his bedside table. Now here's a set of baseball cards and over here we have an autographed picture of Ted Williams."

She looked around her shop. "What type of gift did you have in mind?"

"I know very little about children. I'm afraid I don't know much about what kids like. I do know he's going to have a long recovery, probably more than a month." He kept turning back to the figurine of the family.

"How much money do you plan to spend?" she asked

"I will spend whatever it takes for this boy," he said quietly.

She stood looking at him for a minute saying nothing.

"If money is no object, I have the perfect idea. Julia, Julia, come here," she called to her companion.

"Meet Andy Mellon. Andy, meet, Julia."

They shook hands.

"Andy has a need for a special gift for Hobie. I'm going to take him shopping. Can you lock up tonight?"

"Of course, I can. Good luck."

"Where are we going?" he asked as they walked to her car.

"You'll see."

They headed out for the highway.

Once there, she headed to Toy's R Us. "I think we'll find something here that he'll like. He's going to be in bed or confined in a chair for a while, so we want something he can use from there. I'd suggest a video game. All the kids play them. Or maybe a computer game. Does he have a computer......?" She paused - thinking. Then she smiled. "You said money was no object. I know the perfect gift. Let's go." She hurried from the store with Andy close behind her. They headed for the electronic store.

"Show us your smartest smart phone," she said to the man behind the counter.

"Who is your customer?" the salesman asked.

"A young boy confined to bed," she told him.

"We have these models that would work quite nicely," he said as he presented a tray of phones for Andy to see.

"I guess I'm way behind the times," Andy said as he viewed the phones in front of him.

"You mean you don't have a smart phone," Sarah asked

"I guess I don't. Here's my cell phone," he said as he showed her his phone.

"You need a smart phone. Smart phones are wonderful. You have a way to make calls, play games, look up information, be a camera, give directions, pay your bills, well, they just do everything. Show us your selection," she told the man behind the counter.

Some forty-five minutes later, Andy and Sarah walked out of the store with two phones; one for Hobie and one for Andy.

"You just spent a lot of money," she said.

"He might be in his bed for a long time. I'll do anything I can or buy anything I can to help him have a full recovery."

"It was very thoughtful for you to have the monthly billing sent to you."

"He's been through so much already and he has a long recovery ahead."

"Still, it is a very thoughtful gift. And could turn out to be very expensive. When are you going to give it to him?"

"I'm going back to Chicago this weekend. I'll take it then."

When they arrived back at Sarah's store they could see that Julia had closed the shop for the night.

"The shop is closed. Do you have plans for the evening or do you have time for dinner?" he asked her.

"Dinner sounds great. But let's go dutch. You just spent a lot of money."

"Nope, let's go somewhere nice. Not a diner. You've been so very nice to help me with this gift. I owe you a nice dinner."

"The Lake House is the nicest place in town but sometimes you need a reservation. Let's go to Russells just down the street. We can walk there."

Andy helped Sarah out of the car and together they walked to Russells.

"Tell me about you," he asked after they had ordered.

"Not much to say. I live here in Nuna Lake and hope to spend the rest of my life here."

"Ever married?" he asked.

"Nope. Had a long time affair with a man who wanted to live in Florida but I can't leave Nuna Lake. We finally called it quits a couple of years ago. But I'm a person who doesn't depend on someone else to make them happy. Happiness has to come from within. How about you, are you now or were you ever married?"

"I was for almost a year. That was a long time ago"

"Do you miss her?"

"No, not at all. It was not the happiest of times."

What brought you to Nuna Lake?"

"I saw a picture in a magazine and decided to come here."

"That must have been the spread on Rose and her lawn mowers."

"It was, indeed."

The waiter arrived with appetizers. They concentrated on the food and made small talk while they ate. They walked back to the store where their cars were parked.

"Thank you so much for your help with the phones, and thank you for having dinner with me," Andy said.

"Well, thank you for dinner. It was a fun way to end my day. And I do think Hobie will love his phone. It was a very thoughtful gift," she answered.

"May I, ah, is it okay if I ask you to go to dinner another time," he said, suddenly feeling very stupid.

"Of course," she answered. "I'd like that."

As he walked away Andy felt like he was walking on air one minute and like a fifteen year-old asking for his first date the next minute. *What am I doing? What am I doing?* he thought. Then the answer came to him as if it were written in front of him. *I'm behaving like a normal man for my age. I am behaving in a normal manner, not hiding in some New York apartment. I'm living a normal life.*

"I hope you have had dinner already," Harry said when Andy arrived home.

"Actually, I did. Sarah was so nice to help me that I took her to dinner at Russells. She was so helpful. Let me show you what I got for Hobie. We ended up at an electronic store and got him a smart phone."

"I've heard of them. I guess they do everything," Henry said.

"Let me show you."

Andy showed Harry all the features of the phone. "And I even bought one for me. My old phone is an antique." He showed Harry his old phone.

Harry started to laugh. "Even my phone is a little more up-to-date. You'll love your new phone. But I do have news for you. My daughter is coming tomorrow to take me for a vacation at her house. I know I'll miss you, miss having meals with you. But she has convinced me to go and visit her for a while."

"I think that's nice. She loves you, I can tell from her constant phone calls and cards she sends. I'll take good care of your house. It's been a while since I lived alone. These last few weeks have flown by. I'll miss you. But at least we can talk on the phone."

"I'll be leaving this afternoon. It's a quick trip so Angela can travel with me."

Even on the first day Andy really did miss Harry. The house seemed big and empty. *How did I ever live in that big New York apartment for so long all by myself?* He thought about Hobie a lot and looked forward to his visit to Chicago to see him. He planned to leave after work on Friday night and spend the weekend there. The phone reports he got each day were encouraging. Hobie had regained consciousness, and the doctors were already planning the surgery on his legs. After work on Friday, he headed for Chicago and the hospital. He had a smile on his face. He knew Hobie would like his new smart phone.

Judy was sitting in a chair in the hallway right outside Hobie's door when he arrived. She had been crying; her hair was disheveled. She started to cry again when she saw Andy.

"Is it Hobie? Is he worse? Do we need…?"

"No, no, no," she interrupted. "He wants his dad. I had to tell him his dad was gone. He says I'm lying and won't let me come in the room. I don't know what to do."

Andy didn't know what to do either. He surprised himself by remaining calm. "Let me talk to the boy. He's had time to adjust to the news by now. He's strong like his dad. He'll be okay." Andy went immediately into the room.

"Hi, there," he said in what he hoped was a happy voice.

"My dad is dead," Hobie said in a lost melancholy voice.

"Yes, I know," Andy said in what he hoped was a kind voice. "It was a terrible accident. You nearly died too. But you didn't. You were injured but now you're getting better. You will need to be strong now for your mother. She's going to need your strength. She needs to know you'll be there to take care of her."

Andy's voice was shaking as he talked. He had never done anything like this in his life. *What if Hobie starts to relapse, what if…?*

Hobie turned his back on Andy and said nothing. He stared at the wall. Finally, Hobie turned to Andy.

"Is my mother still here or has she gone home?"

"I'll look to see. Do you want to see her?"

"I guess."

Andy went to the door. Judy was sitting in a chair with her head in her hands.

"He wants to see you."

87

Judy rushed to the room, and then stopped at the door.

"Sorry, Mom." The voice was very quiet.

"Oh, Hobie, I love you so much...."

Andy quietly stepped out of the room.

A nurse came by. "What are you doing here? Are you here for the night shift?"

"His mother is telling him goodbye. He now knows about his father's death. He didn't accept the news too well."

"What child would accept such news? Are you sleeping in the chair tonight? I'll bring you coffee and a blanket." She went on her rounds.

Andy sat there with his head in his hands. He wasn't sure what to do next. He finally decided to do nothing for a few minutes, then peeked into the room and saw Judy sitting on the bed, holding Hobie as best she could. Then he heard Hobie talking.

"I'm going to be okay, Mom. I'll take care of you. Go home now. Take care of Katie. She needs you, too."

With tears streaming down her face, Judy kissed her son goodnight and came out of the room. Andy put his arms around her and let her cry. Then she left to go take care of her other child.

Andy went into Hobie's room. "You were really a man taking care of your mom," he said. Hobie turned to the wall. Andy didn't know whether to go or stay. He finally sat down in the chair which would become his bed for the night.

"I had a good dad. I'll really miss him." Andy heard a quiet little voice, turned to the wall, speaking.

"I'll miss him too," Andy said. "He was the first friend I made when I came to Nuna Lake. He and your mother were so kind to me. They welcomed me into your family. I never had a family like that."

"You had a mom and dad. Did they die?"

"I never knew either one of them."

"How come?"

"Well, my dad was a soldier in the Vietnam War. He died there. He had met my mother there. She was a nurse. She died shortly after I was born. But I had wonderful grandparents who took me into their arms and their home."

"It must be terrible to never know your dad or mom."

"My grandparents were very good to me."

"You must miss your folks a lot."

"No, actually, you can't miss what you didn't have. I never knew either one. But I loved and missed my grandparents when they died."

"At least I have a mom."

"Yes, you do. And she loves you so much. She needs you to be strong for her."

Nothing more was said for a few minutes. Andy sat their quietly. He wanted to say something to comfort this child but didn't know what to say. He thought of a lot of old cliques that people say at funerals but knew they would not be appropriate. So he sat quietly.

Finally Hobie started to talk. He talked about his dad teaching him how to throw a ball, how to ride a bike, how to…well, he kept talking. Andy sat quietly, listening. Then Hobie started to cry for his father. Andy moved to the side of the bed, trying to sit there among all the tubes and lines still connected to Hobie's body, to comfort him.

The nurse came into the room with a blanket and cup of coffee for Andy. She saw Andy trying to comfort the boy. She gave him a sign with her thumb and forefinger making an O that let him know she understood. She quietly left the room. Andy suddenly had a thought. *This is the first time I have really put my arms around anyone.* Maybe the last time was when he and Gretchen were first married. They certainly had not made love much after that. He felt he wanted to protect this child. He tried holding him a little closer.

Finally, Andy felt Hobie's body relax. He gently laid Hobie back down on the bed and moved to the chair. He had never felt so inadequate. He had never felt so alone.

Andy was awakened the next morning by the early staff medical attendants starting their rounds. Their bright cheery voices made Andy want to hide under the blanket. But he was anxious to see what kind of a mood Hobie would be in.

"Are you awake," he heard Hobie ask.

"I think so," Andy answered, trying to get awake.

"Is it true I have to have more surgery? When can I go home?"

"I believe they want to do some repair work on your leg so you can walk again. Then you can go home."

"Who's taking care of my mother now? Who's taking care of Katie? I need to know they're okay."

"Your Mom and Katie are with your grandparents and Aunt Karen and Aunt Sandy." He was quiet for a minute.

"I miss them. I miss Katie even if she is a pest."

"Why don't you call them? Is there a phone in this room?" He pretended to look around the room. "What's this package over here? Oh, I know what it is. It's a present for you."

"For me?"

"Yea, something to do while you're still in bed."

Andy handed Hobie the package with the phone.

Hobie started to carefully unwrap it, then seeing a picture on the box, excitedly tore off the wrapping.

"It's a phone. It's a phone. Is it really for me? Is it really mine?"

"I think it is. Let's look at it together." Andy moved to the bed. Taking the phone from the box, he said. "I believe that if you push that little icon your mother will answer her cell phone."

Hobie pushed the icon.

"Hello."

"Hi, Mom, it's me."

"Hobie? Hobie. Is that you?"

"Andy gave me a phone."

"My mother's crying," Hobie told Andy.

"Tell her how much better you are today."

"Andy said to tell you I'm much better."

"Oh, Hobie, oh Hobie. Here's Katie. She wants to say hello."

The two children talked for a minute then the nurse came into the room.

"I have to go now. Talk to you later," Hobie said as he closed the call. Then he turned to the nurse and said, "See what Andy brought me."

The nurse, very pleased to see him so enthused, made a big fuss about the phone and then wheeled his bed out of the room. He took his phone with him.

Andy stood there, ready to cry. He had never, never, never given anyone anything and got that kind of a response. Hobie really loved the phone. *Thank you, thank you, Sarah, for thinking of it.*

Andy decided to go to the cafeteria for breakfast while Hobie was gone for tests. He was joined by David Hass who sat down with a cup of coffee.

"I stopped by the business office. They told me you are submitting no charges."

"So"

"David, you are a very good man."

"I've done it before."

"But you did it so quietly that no one knows about it."

"You are one of my best friends. I'm doing it for you. And for Nuna Lake. I've never heard of a town like that one."

"When things settle down, find a new piece of equipment you'd like to have. Money is no object. I mean it. I owe you big-time."

"Your little buddy is flying high today. They could hardly get him to put down the phone for his tests. That was a thoughtful gift you gave him. It was good to see him like a happy little boy. His recovery is remarkable. We'll do some repair work on his leg next week and he'll be almost ready to go home. Of course, he'll have to have therapy about twice a week. I hope that won't put too much strain on his mother," David said.

"She's a strong woman. And she's got good family support. And good town support. I can't believe Nuna Lake. It's an amazing place."

"I never did get all the details of how you got there."

Just then his buzzer went off and David said goodbye and rushed off.

Andy had not been a church-goer since he lived with his grandparents, but he took a few minutes that morning to stop in the chapel at the hospital to say thank you and have a few minutes of meditation.

When Hobie returned to the room he was even more excited by his new phone.

"One of the guys down there said this was a super phone. He showed me how to take a picture. I took pictures of everyone. Want to see them?"

"Of course I do," Andy said. The next hour was spent looking at the phone, looking at the pictures of everyone in the treatment room. He then did a lot of silly poses so Hobie could take his picture, and he took pictures of Hobie being silly. The morning passed quickly.

That afternoon Andy showed Hobie how to bring up games. Hobie was thrilled to be playing games. For the first time since the accident, Andy breathed a sigh of relief. It did appear that Hobie was on the way to recovery. He owed Sarah a lot for thinking of the phone. He decided to call her.

"Hi, I took a chance calling you at the store. I didn't know if you would be there."

"Yes, I'm here and I'm glad you called. Did Hobie like the phone? Is he able to use it?"

"He loves his phone. He hasn't put it down. I showed him how to use: the phone, the camera, and the games. He's taken a picture of everyone who has come in his room." Andy paused. "It was the perfect gift at the perfect time. His mother had just told him about the death of his father. He was angry and upset. We finally got him calmed down for the night. I gave him the phone this morning. It was a big hit. Even the staff that came in the room had their picture taken. They were great. They horsed around with him, even making me take their picture with him. You can't believe how much it has encouraged him. Even I believe he can be completely healed now. How can I ever thank you for thinking of it?"

"Well, actually that's my job. Finding the right gift for the person at the right time. Usually I try hard because it means a sale for me. It was nice to be a part of doing something for someone that doesn't involve the store."

"What can I do to say thank you?" he asked.

"I'll think of something."

"I'll call you when I get home."

Andy pushed the end button on his phone.

Chapter 10

Andy returned home to an empty house. No Harry there to fuss over him and ask about his day. No Harry there to give him advice on living a full life. No Harry there to remember the wonderful days with his beloved Millie. Andy liked hearing about it all. He realized he was feeling lonely. He couldn't remember feeling this way ever before. Or was it this feeling that led him to leave New York and head for Nuna Lake. Maybe. He wished he had someone to talk to about his trip, about Hobie's healing, about..... well, maybe just everyday things.

The next morning when he arrived at work the secretary told him Mike wanted to see him but was out of the office. She'd call him when Mike arrived.

A moment of dread came over Andy. His first thought was that Mike knows who Andy really is and will ask him to leave. Should he just offer to quit first? He was making friends all over town. Could he find another job so he could stay here?

With a sad face he hunted out Gabe who would assign him for the day.

"Hey, there, glad to see you back," Gabe said. "Why the long face? I heard Hobie is doing great. And I heard about your gift to him. It was the right thing at the right time."

"I hear Mike wants to see me."

"Yea, he does. I think I just saw his car pull in the parking lot. Let's go see him."

Together they walked to the office. Andy hadn't felt this way for weeks – well, maybe since he left New York. He was certain that Mike was going to fire him. Still, a lot of the help were students who had returned to school. This place might need him. Well, it would all be over soon.

"Hey, I hear we have good news about Hobie" Mike said when he entered the room.

"I think he's made a turn-around. Dr. Hass is going to do some minor surgery this week. Then it's all rehab."

"You certainly have been a good friend to Tom's family and to all the citizens of Nuna Lake. Even your gift to him – that phone – made Hobie come alive. Can we help you pay for the phone?"

"That's not necessary but I can't take real credit for a phone. Harry suggested I ask Sarah for ideas. She was very helpful. She even helped me choose the phone."

"This town wouldn't know what to do if Sarah left town," Gabe said.

"Enough chitchat. Let's talk business," Mike said.

"For the first time in twenty-some years, Martha needs some time off. She will be out for about six or eight weeks. You know she oversees all the plantings, does a lot of the buying, and also oversees the testing we do in our labs. She takes care of the inside business and Gabe takes care of the outside business. She has recommended that you take over for her while she is gone. Everything in there is very detailed and she thinks you're the person for the job. I know you indicated to me you might not be here very long. Would you be able to stay long enough for her to have the time off? Would you be willing to accept this responsibility?"

Andy sat there in a daze. He had let himself think he was about to be fired, that everyone would know of his secrets and now this! His hands began to shake and he felt unable to speak.

"Ah, ah, I could do anything she tells me to do but I certainly don't have the knowledge or expertise to do her job. She has so much knowledge."

"She thinks you're the person for the job. I'll be here. Gabe will be here. We agree with Martha. You're detail minded. That's one skill that's needed for this job. Everything you do in the lab has to be written down. Martha is having a hip replaced, but will be available by phone if you need help."

"Yes, yes, I'll try to do the job," he stuttered in a soft voice. "I thought you were going to fire me."

"Why would you think that?" Gabe asked with a smile.

"I guess, I guess because I drifted into town only planning to be here a few weeks."

"So you just stay a while longer," Mike said. "Martha is down in the lab now waiting to hear your answer. Why don't you go and tell her you'll do it? Oh, incidentally, the job pays double your usual wages. Welcome aboard."

He left to find Martha.

"Welcome back. I hear Hobie is really improving now. Let me really show you around the lab, not the quick course you got your first day," she said.

He started to jot down notes of things he shouldn't forget. At times he felt almost over-whelmed by the responsibility he would be given. But in a way, he almost welcomed the challenge. *Mike must think I'm capable or he wouldn't trust me,* he thought.

"I came to you with shakes and shudders," he told Martha.

"I know. It's because I'm like a grizzly mama bear about this section," she said with a smile. "You'll do fine. Are you sure you never did this kind of work before. You have a great eye for detail."

"I've been around plants all my life but I've taken very little complete care of any. Well, I did have a small vegetable garden when I was in the 4-H club. I must have been about twelve years old. Does that count?"

"Only if you loved the plants. These are my babies. I'll be a bit jealous if someone else is good to them," she said with a smile. "Plan to spend the rest of the week with me and I'll teach you my routine."

"See you tomorrow," he said as he left.

But his joy was not to last. He began to feel like he was a phony. Everyone in Nuna Lake accepted him as he pretended to be. But he is Andrew Mellon, a man who can buy and sell anyone; he's a faker – trying to live the life of an everyday man. If he told them who he really was they would probably ride him out of town on a rail. He sat in a chair for a time, reliving his decision to…well, try to be something he's not. What would people say if they knew the real Andrew Mellon? The multi-millionaire posing as a poor working man…wearing old clothes and driving an old car. He sat quietly pondering if he should admit who he was. He wished Harry was here to talk with, but he was still with his daughter.

His cell phone rang.

"Andy, it's me, Hobie; I'm coming home. I'm coming home."

"I know. You'll be here soon."

"No, you don't understand. I'll be there tomorrow. Here's the doctor."

"Dr. Hass here," Mike heard his friend's voice on the phone. "This young man has progressed so well it's a miracle. It's time for him to be closer to home. You have a very good hospital near you. I believe Hobie can continue his therapy there so his mother can return to her home and still visit him."

"Is this for real?" Andy asked his friend.

"Yep, it is. The ambulance plane is available tomorrow morning. We'll have a nurse make the trip with him so you don't need to come back. The hospital in Sprucedale will follow the instructions for his therapy. He'll need to be in the hospital for a week or ten days. They are well trained there to help him. He's had a remarkable recovery. I told his mother and she is leaving right away to prepare for his homecoming. I wasn't sure we could save him for a while. I'm sure a lot of prayers were said for him. His therapy will be pretty intense so try to keep him encouraged. You know, Andy, when I saw that boy for the first time I almost didn't even want to try to help him. He's a remarkable little boy. I'm a big believer in a strong support system and I think that's what helped him. Oh, by the way, I'm charging the ambulance plane to you."

"David, how can I ever repay you for all you've done?"

"I make good money and do not need to be paid for it. Your town of Nuna Lake must be a very caring community. I've never seen anything like it."

"I know you love your work. That's what makes you so good at being a doctor. I owe you big time. I did not expect the town to chip in to pay his expenses. I say this honestly and seriously: call me when the next new piece of equipment comes along. It will be a small payment on a very large debt."

Andy made his way to tell the others the good news about Hobie.

Mike immediately said, 'You must meet them at the airport. Take all the time you need to get them settled. Maybe we should broadcast the good news over the PA System. The whole town has been praying for him."

Andy stood there, unable to speak. Then he said quietly. "This community has healed Hobie. I've never known of a community like this." He also thought, but did not say it — *This town is healing me. I know I'm a changed man. Now I just need help to let people know what a fake I've been.*

Chapter 11

The next couple of weeks were busy ones for Andy. He started his new job in the lab and had to admit he loved being there. He arrived early and stayed late. He still found time for Hobie each day. After one week in the hospital, they sent Hobie home. Andy felt like he should help Judy, but she seemed to be doing okay. One night he had stopped by to see Hobie after work, and found Judy knee deep in paper work trying to get Tom's affairs in order. Her neighbor, an accountant who lived a few doors away. was helping her. Andy learned the man was a widower with two school age children. He learned Judy would let the man's children come to her house after school in exchange for his help in settling Tom's estate. Hobie and the children crowded around Andy and insisted he play a game with them. He was glad to see the children were getting on with their life.

But how was he going to get on with his life. Sometimes his past life loomed over him like a large dark cloud, but mostly he was able to keep it buried in the back of his mind.

He arrived home from work the next night really missing Harry. There was no one to tell about all the interesting research Mike had going. And there was no one with his food on the table or have his hot coffee ready each morning. He really missed Harry. The house seemed big and empty. He decided to call him.

"Harry, this is Andy. Haven't heard from you this week. How are you? When are you coming home? I miss you."

"Andy, the news is not good. I fell last week and broke my hip. At my age that's bad news."

"Why didn't you call me? Are you in the hospital? Is your doctor any good? Is…"

"Slow down, Andy. My daughter is taking good care of me. I'm in a convalescent home trying to recover. But they won't let me come home. I'm worried about something. Remember that paper I had you sign before I left?"

"You mean the power of attorney?"

"Yes. Will you please get my bank statements and make sure the utilities are paid. And taxes are due on the house. Will you make sure they are paid? There is money in my bank account."

"I'll be glad to do that. But I miss you. Tell me how you really are."

"Pretty uncomfortable. My daughter wanted me to come to her house, but I insisted on coming here. Millie and I made a vow to not be a burden to our children."

"Harry, you're not a burden to your children. You're very independent."

"I'm a burden to my daughter who is doing her best to look after me, look after her husband who has cancer, work at a full time job, and take care of her family. I want to come home but I have to admit I'm not able to do the things I could before. But I still have sense enough to know when I need help. Right now I need help with paying my taxes."

"Don't give it another thought. I'll send you the receipt tomorrow."

"Is everything okay there? How is Hobie? How are you? Are you finding Nuna Lake friendly enough that you want to stay there?"

"I think Nuna Lake is a wonderful place to live. I do want to stay longer. Let me tell you about work." Andy told Harry about his work, about Hobie, and about how the town was recovering from the big accident, about the waitress at their favorite diner being engaged, how everyone missed Harry and wanted him back.

Then Harry said, "I'm so tired right now. I want to come home. I want to go that place on the highway that they build for seniors. My friends, the ones that are still alive, are there. I want to come home. Hobie had an ambulance plane take him to Chicago. Couldn't I get one of those planes to bring me home?"

"You said you're tired. I'll get the information you want. Let's hang up now. I'll call you tomorrow," Andy said as he pressed the end button on his phone. He sat there quietly, remembering their good times of the summer, the wisdom that Harry always had. Andy knew Harry must be in his late eighties or early nineties. Would he ever recover? He thought about the town. Everyone loves Harry. If people knew they would send Harry cards. But how do you tell a town about something like this. He decided to call Mike.

"Hello, this is Rose."

'Hi, this is Andy. I just talked to Harry. He's broken his hip."

"Oh, no," she cried and then said "Let me get Mike on the line." He heard her tell Mike to pick up the phone.

"This is Mike," he said.

"Mike, I have bad news about Harry. He fell and broke his hip."

'Oh, no," he said.

After Andy told them the details, he asked for advice. "How can we let the town know so they can encourage him with mail? What do you think about moving him back here? Should I encourage or discourage him?"

"I was just on my way out the door to a meeting with the Chamber of Commerce. Everyone will know before bedtime. But what can we do to help Harry?" he asked. "I'll think on this and we'll talk tomorrow."

Andy sat in the chair a long time. *Will Harry recover? Will he, Andy, need to move from Harry's house? Would he have survived Nuna Lake if Harry had not taken him in?* He didn't think so. Should he go to Arizona to be with Harry now or would the family find him intrusive? What would Harry's children say to do? What if...

He sat there quietly and thought about what a good man Harry was. Then he paced the floor. Was it right to bring him home away from his family? Was it right to leave him there where he knew no one and only his very busy daughter could come to see him? He sat quietly thinking...thinking that Harry had become his family. It had been a long time since Andy thought of that word – family. He missed Harry and wanted him home.

His cell phone rang.

"Hi, this is Sarah. I'm just leaving the Chamber of Commerce meeting. Tell me it's not true. Tell me Harry is fine."

"I'm so glad you called. I need a friend to talk to," Andy told her. "Yes, it is true, he broke his hip. But more than that, he wants to come home to the convalescent center attached to Sprucedale Hospital."

"Well, I know why. His three best friends are there. He visits them every week to play rummy or chess with them. He needs to come home. This is where his friends are. We need him back here."

"I didn't know that. I thought I knew all about him."

"None of us ever know everything about everybody. I volunteer at the home one afternoon a week. That's how I know."

"Sarah, you're a very good person."

"Nuna Lake is my town. I love everyone who lives here. I think we should bring Harry home. His daughter Angela and I were best friends many years ago. I spent many hours in their home as a child and young girl. Mike and I talked it over and we think I should be the one to call Angela and tell her about Harry's call to you. I think I should do it tonight. I do know Angela's going through a rough time right now. Her husband is very sick. She must be having a hard time to keep up with things."

"I know Harry doesn't want to be a burden to his daughter," Andy said.

"I imagine she's run pretty ragged by now, trying to be at home to help her husband and at the hospital to help her dad. We need to help her too. That's why I called you. Is it too late for me to stop by your house tonight to see how we make this happen?"

"It's not too late."

"Do you have a coffee pot? I didn't have dinner tonight and I'd like to stop at Burger King and pick up a burger, if that's okay with you."

"Pick up two burgers. I didn't eat tonight either. Somehow I just didn't feel hungry. But a burger sounds good. I'll put on the coffee."

"I've had a hard time getting interested in food now that Harry's not here to share it," Andy told Sarah when she arrived with the food.

"Let's sit at the kitchen table. That coffee smells wonderful. Now let me tell you what Mike and I think. We think Harry should come back to Nuna Lake. At the home he'll be with all his old friends and I think he'll heal more quickly. We have good doctor's here. And he'll have a constant stream of friends to encourage him. Mike thinks I should be the one to tell Angela about our plans."

"Do you think she'll agree to it?"

"Not at first, but if I know Angela she'll come around. She's going through a rough time with her husband right now. Down deep I think she'll realize this is the best thing not only for Andy but for her too. Her sister and brother both are living out of the country and I know she needs help. Angela has a daughter who lives about fifty miles from her who is trying to help but it's a bad time for them."

"Are you going to think about this overnight?"

"No, why put it off. It's still early evening in Arizona. I'll call her now." She reached for her cell phone.

"Want me to leave the room while you call?"

"Andy, we'll need you to make the arrangements. You need to know what is being said."

Andy was a bit shocked. When had anyone ever told him he was needed?

"I'll fix us a fresh cup of coffee," he said.

"I'll put you on speaker phone," Angela said.

He listened while Sarah talked to Angela – about how Angela was holding up, about Angela's husband, and then about Harry.

"Angela, you've really got your hands full now. Harry is worried about you. He thinks he's a bother. I know he's not. And I know you always could multi-task better than everyone else. But Andy called him tonight and he told Andy he wants to come home."

"That's not a surprise to me. He does love Nuna Lake. He and Mom didn't want to leave it even to visit us."

"Would you consider letting him come home? He'd be surrounded by his Nuna Lake family, which means almost every one in town. There is a convalescent home for seniors attached to the Sprucedale Hospital. I hear they give excellent care there. He'd be there with his two best friends. Harry has been going out to play cards or checkers or chess with them each week. I think it might be good for Harry. Then you can concentrate on helping your husband get well."

"I told my mother I'd look after Daddy."

"And you will. You'll be putting him in a place where he'll get good care and where he'll be surrounded by friends. This town really misses him."

"Let me call you back tomorrow. I want to talk with my brother and sister. They have been trying to make arrangements to come home from overseas more quickly. I'll call you tomorrow. Is there a good time to call?"

"I'll be at the store all day tomorrow. Call me there."

"Well, I did my best," Sarah told Andy. "I think she'll say yes. Then it's up to you to make this happen."

"I'm up to the challenge. Should I wait till she says yes to make the arrangements?"

"Maybe we should."

"You'll call me as soon as you hear anything?"

"Of course. I'd better head for home," she said. "Thanks for the coffee and the conversation. I'll call you as soon as I hear anything." She slung her purse over her shoulder and started out the door.

He came out the door after her. "I'll follow you home to make sure you get there safely."

"Of course you won't. I'm often on the road at night. I live less than fifteen minutes away."

"You shouldn't be on the road alone at night."

"You forget I'm used to being alone. I live alone, I travel alone …"

"I want to see you safely home so I can sleep tonight," he told her.

"It really isn't necessary. But it's a beautiful gesture on your part. How about this: I will call you as soon as I get home. If I don't call you, you can come looking for me."

"Promise?"

"Promise."

"Lock your car doors," he told her.

He paced the floor. The next fifteen minutes seemed to be an eternity. Finally, the phone rang. He answered it immediately.

"Are you home?"

"Safely home. I'll call you tomorrow."

"Do you have my cell number?"

"Yes, I wrote it down."

"Well…Thanks for a pleasant evening. Good night."

With a smile on his face, Andy headed for bed. *What a pleasant evening I had. Sarah's really nice. And caring. She must be very busy at work but not to busy to help her friends.* Andy slept well that night.

Sarah didn't sleep so well. She was confused and…When had any man cared if she got home okay? What man would be concerned about an old man like Andy cared about Harry? She thought of the man who had been in her life for some years, the one who moved to Florida. He didn't care enough to stay in Nuna Lake even though he knew how much she loved the little town. She had thought she'd spend her life with him even if he didn't believe in marriage. Thank goodness she still had enough common sense and pride to send him on his way. Somehow, down deep she knew he would never want to get married. That was okay with her. She had a rich, full life. But, she had to admit, she had been surprised when he left her. It took her some time to get over it.

Chapter 12

Andy went to work the next morning feeling, well, he felt good. He had plans for the day. He was going to arrange for Harry to come home. He knew Angela would say it was okay. He decided to send for his own plane to bring Harry home. They could easy remove a seat or two so Harry could lay down. He decided to call the airport in New York to arrange the flight. He'd have them stop in Nuna Lake to pick him up and head for Arizona. They'd pick up Harry and bring him home. He felt good about what he was going to do. But then a cloud appeared over his head. How would he explain his generous offer? He sat quietly, pondering a scheme to explain how he made it happen. *No,* he thought. *It's time to end this charade. I can't sneak around any more. I will tell Mike the truth as soon as I get to work.* He knew this might change everything; people would see him differently. But he knew it was the right thing to do. He still has his penthouse in New York. Maybe he can find a way to live a different style of life than he had before.

"Morning, Andy," Gabe said when Andy walked in the door. "I'm on my way to meet with Mike. Come along and tell us how you and Sarah made out with Angela."

They walked into Mike's office. Andy told them about Sarah's call to Angela. "We're waiting to hear back this morning." He paused and then said. "I need to talk to you both. Can you spare me a few minutes."

"Of course. I'll have Jenna bring us coffee" After Jenna brought in the coffee, Andy swallowed hard and began.

"I have never lied to you but I still have not been truthful. My name is Andy Mellon and I am from New York. I have never been arrested or even questioned by the police. But I am not a poor drifter who wandered into Nuna Lake. I came here with a purpose. My name is Andy Mellon but most people know me as Andrew Mellon, New York City wealthy investor. I own a penthouse there with a roof top garden and a beautiful rose bush that is strictly experimental. Do you want to hear more or do you want me to leave now?" he asked the men.

"Why not tell us everything," Mike said quietly.

"I have a lot of acquaintances and a lot of money but I became a recluse. I had two good friends who did worry about me, one was my housekeeper named Mima, and the other was Marvin Hartley, the man who experimented with roses. You may have heard of him."

"Of course I've heard of him," Mike said. "Everyone has heard of him...wait a minute. I read about the new rose he's working on. Are you...you must be the man funding his research."

"I am. He does the work and I get the credit."

"I want to hear everything about him and the new rose. It must be magnificent."

"I'll tell you anything you want to know. But first, let me tell you about how I came to Nuna Lake. I had no pleasure in life except for my roses. I rarely left my house, which was a rooftop penthouse. I had purchased it when I married. I had been extremely lucky in my investments when computers and the internet were introduced. My marriage was short and sweet. She spent a lot of money and left after a few months for a former count from Italy who had even more money than I did. I hired a good investor who made my fund grow. I spent very little money. I quit going to work. I became a recluse and rarely left the house. The only pleasure I had in my life was working with Marvin on my roses. We had many ups and downs experimenting with different feeding patterns. But enough about the roses. One day I picked up a glossy magazine (one the decorator had deemed acceptable for my position). It was Classic Homes, the one featuring Nuna Lake."

"But that was almost two years ago," Mike said.

"I had paid no attention to what was happening in my penthouse. I went to a few social events with old acquaintances. The only two people I really had in my life was my housekeeper who came each morning and Marvin Hartley. When I saw the pictures and read of Nuna Lake, well, I guess I felt compelled to come here. I wanted to change my life and be part of …. well, I guess you could say I wanted a life. I told no one. I bought an old car (the housekeeper's daughter's old one), went to the Salvation Army for clothes and started off. I made my way here. When I met you the first day, Mike, and you hired me I thought I had died and gone to heaven. The only dark cloud I have hanging over me is that you might feel I have pulled a con on you, pretending to be needy when I was not. Now that you do know everything if you want me to leave, I will."

"Do you want to leave?" Mike asked.

"No, I love my life here. I feel like I could live here forever. But I learned that when you have money, life sometimes changes. People have a million "good causes" that need money. I have a very good stock broker who keeps making me more money. I have a business manager who watches my spending. I have a limousine and a driver to take me anywhere I want to go. I even have my own plane and a pilot to take me anywhere. I didn't want people to know I had money; it sometimes ends in a lost friendship. But how can I have a friend or be a friend if I am living a lie."

The room was quiet. Finally, Mike spoke. "I know you don't know Gabe or me too well. I appreciate your telling us about your past life. I know of no reason either one of us would find it necessary to tell anyone. I will admit I was surprised when the town collected so much money for Hobie. We had a lot of fifty and hundred dollar bills in the collection jars."

"I didn't know how else to contribute. I think the people of Nuna Lake are just very giving people," Andy said. "But I will confess one thing. Dr. David Hass, who operated on Hobie, was my roommate in college. I do believe he is the only one who could have saved Hobie. I called him. I expected to pay for everything, I believe he told you he had a benefactor who would pay the bill, but you spoke up and said 'Nuna Lake takes care of its own'".

Mike spoke quietly. "I was surprised but thought maybe lady luck was with us, when he came to the hospital. I had heard of him and knew he was very good. But I've never known of anyone coming to Nuna Lake to fish," Mike said quietly. They sat very still for a couple of minutes.

'You have ended a mystery for me. When I hired you I didn't expect you to last a week, but you surprised me. Martha wouldn't trust her lab to any one but you."

Gabe spoke. "I agree with Mike. I think this conversation should be kept private. I imagine people with money get bombarded with requests for help. I know Mike won't say anything to anyone and neither will I. But even people with money need help sometimes. We'll be there for you. And now we'd better get to work. Come on and show me how Martha's babies in the lab are doing today. I have to go see Martha this afternoon."

At that moment Andy felt like he could cry. Or maybe he could fly to the moon. But he simply reached out and gave each man a hug and said simply, "Thank you."

He got more and more anxious to hear from Sarah about Harry. Then he tried to remember the time difference. Finally, his phone finally rang.

"Did I get you at a bad time?" Sarah asked. "I just heard back from Angela. She talked things over with her husband; she called her sister and brother. After thinking things over. Angela decided to accept Nuna Lake's offer to let him return home. I called the hospital in Arizona about what needs he might have for the trip, and I called the convalescence home here to make sure they have room for him. It's a go all the way."

"Then let's make arrangements to move him tomorrow. I have a private plane available with seats we can make into a bed."

"That's going to cost a fortune. Would a medical plane be cheaper?"

The truth or the lie. Andy didn't know which to tell.

"I got this covered. Harry has been so good to me. We can make the trip in one day if the weather stays nice. Tell the hospital we should be there before noon their time. Ask them to arrange transport to the airport. I'll call them when I get the details."

"Are you sure you can do all this?" she asked.

"Mike told me to take what time I need."

"Someone just came in the store and I'm working alone this morning. I got to go now. Talk to you later."

Andy called the airport in New York, told them to prepare two or three seats of his plane into a bed and to be at the Nuna Lake airport early the next morning to pick him up. They would fly to Arizona. They would pick up a passenger. They would make a return trip later in the day to Nuna Lake so if they need two pilots, bring one along. He knew his plane was big enough for all of them. It had been a long time since he had used his plane. He also realized that his money made all of this possible. Would he ever realize that his money can be a good thing instead of isolating him from society?

That night Sarah arrived at Andy's. "Let's go over all these plans again. You will go with the plane to Arizona and bring him home."

"Do you want to ride along? There is room for you. Harry likes you a lot and it might comfort him to have you there."

"I'd love to ride along but there's no need to spend the extra money."

"It's a private plane. You would have a chance to see Angela. I imagine she'll be at the airport."

"Who's paying for the private plane?"

"It belongs to a friend of mine." The minute he said it he realized he was starting to lie again. But was there time to tell Sarah everything? What would she think? Before he could change his mind and tell her the truth, she had to leave so he was spared telling his story. While he felt bad about the lie, he felt good about what was happening, and best of all, Harry was coming home.

His mind was full of plans for the next day. He called Sarah. "Got time to grab a bite to eat at Russell's tonight so we can go over our plans for tomorrow."

"Sure thing. I'll meet you there about six if that's okay."

"That's great. See you then."

Andy took a quick shower and put on a new knit shirt he had not worn with his one pair of good slacks. He realized he needed to buy some new clothes. Or does he have clothes in his New York condo he should be wearing? Well, he'd think about that some other day.

Sarah was waiting for him when he arrived. As he sat down he really looked at Sarah. She was a beautiful woman. Her hair was long, a warm brown in color, pulled back into a pony tail. She had on a blue top which was the same shade of her eyes. Her skin was smooth as silk. He really had not noticed her beauty before. Maybe baring his soul to Mike and Gabe was opening his eyes to the world.

"This is a wonderful thing you are doing for Harry," she said. "How did you arrange a private plane so quickly?"

"I waved my magic wand and the plane appeared on the horizon."

"Is that supposed to be funny?"

"Yes."

"Then ha, ha."

"I'll tell you all about it later. Let's order."

"Angela and her family can't believe what Nuna Lake is doing for her dad. The doctor told her he thinks it is exactly what her dad needs. But she is still sad she is not making the trip with him. She is hopeful she can make the trip here in a couple of weeks to make sure he's okay. In the meantime, I promised to be a daughter to Harry."

"Did anyone ever tell you you're a very nice person?"

"Not today."

"Then I'll repeat it – you're a very nice person."

They started to laugh and then looked over the menu.

When they left the restaurant, he said to her, "Can I pick you up in the morning about six thirty to go to the airport. The plane is coming from New York and should be here around seven. We made it early so we can make the return trip the same day. Is everything arranged on this end?"

"The home should have his room ready by noon and his doctor will arrange to see him in the late afternoon or early evening," she said.

"Tomorrow night at this time, we'll have Harry home with us again."

They had a very nice dinner. As they went to leave the restaurant, they saw the donation jar on the counter. There was a sign on it, "Bring Harry Home."

Nuna Lake takes care of its own.

Chapter 13

When he picked up Sarah in the morning, she was excited. "I'm having an adventure today. I don't believe I've ever been on a private plane," she said. "You must have a very good friend who would let you use his plane this way."

"Sarah, there's something I need to tell you. No, it's something I want to tell you. But let's wait till we get on the plane. We'll have time to talk then." He pulled in the parking lot and locked his car. *Someone else to know the truth,* he thought.

The plane was already on the tarmac. Both pilots came to greet Andy with their hands out.

"I feel like it has been forever since we've seen you," the pilot said. "How are you, Mr. Mellon?"

"Joe, truthfully I've never felt or been better. I'd like you to meet my good friend, Sarah. Sarah, this is Joe and this is Hank."

"We've got the bed all ready inside and flight plans are set. Shall we get started right away?" Joe asked.

As they settled in their seats, Sarah wryly said, "I think you got some explaining to do."

"I probably have more to tell you than you want to hear," he said.

"Would you like coffee or anything?" Hank asked.

"Maybe later," Sarah said. She smiled at Hank and said with a note of sarcasm in her voice: "Andy and I have *so* much to talk about."

"Maybe you'd better bring coffee, Hank. I may be in the dog house."

"Coffee coming right up," Hank said.

Hank served the coffee while they were still on the runway.

"Mr. Mellon, what is going on?" Sarah asked, placing great emphasis on his name. "This is definitely not a run-of-the-mill airplane. It's so elegant. I've never been on a plane like this. Did you rob a bank?"

"Just a small one and they didn't catch me." Then quietly he said, "I value our friendship, but you might not want to be friends with me after I tell you all."

"What's going on Andy," she asked quietly.

"My name is Andy Mellon. I came to Nuna Lake because I saw a picture of the town in a magazine. I wanted a new way of life." He paused and then continued.

"For the past twenty years or more, my acquaintances called me Andrew or Mr. Mellon. I guess you could say I am a wealthy investor from New York. I have a stock broker who has made both of us very wealthy. I quit my job and stayed home all day doing nothing. I had riches around me but no person I could really call a friend. One day I bought a used car, clothes from the Salvation Army and took off for Nuna Lake. I only expected to be here for a few days. I wanted to see its beauty, its people, its way of life. I only told one person I was leaving, a very nice lady who came each morning to fix my breakfast and make my bed. I only expected to be gone for a week or a month at the most. The people of Nuna Lake made me one of their own. No one asked questions. Instead of living a lonely life, I began to really live life. The more I lived it, the more I loved it. I have more friends in Nuna Lake than I dreamed possible. I left acquaintances in New York, not friends. Even if I am kicked out of Nuna Lake, I will always value how the people of the town took me in and let me have a new way of life. The only bad thing was that I was living a lie, letting people here think I was some poor drifter who came to town."

"You've been carrying a big secret. I don't think anyone would suspect you are not what you seen." Sarah sat quietly for a few minutes.

Andy said nothing. It was one thing to tell Mike and Gabe, but this woman is the most down-to-earth, self-assured woman he ever met. She depends on no one. Will she tell him to get out of her life after they return home? *Well, maybe it's what I deserve.* They sat quietly for a few minutes and then Sarah spoke.

"How many people know your story?"

"I just told Mike and Gabe yesterday."

"What did they say?"

"Well, they didn't fire me which I thought they would."

"I imagine they feel the story is yours to tell."

After a few more minutes passed she said, "It was you, wasn't it, who put the fifty and hundred dollar bills in the collection pot for Hobie?"

120

"Yes. David Hass was my college friend. I knew he might be the only one who could save Hobie. I called David and asked him to come right away. I expected to pay all Hobie's expenses myself. When David told Mike there was a benefactor to pay Hobie's bill, Mike said 'Nuna Lake takes care of its own.' I knew my help had to be like the rest: given freely and thoughtfully and privately to help him."

"You saved Hobie's life. You must know that."

"I'll take credit for getting David here quickly, but it was Nuna Lake that saved his life."

Joe came to talk to Andy.

"We thought maybe you had moved away. We didn't hear from you all summer. It was so good to hear from you. Even though you didn't use your plane much, we missed seeing you around."

"I have friends in Nuna Lake. Really good friends. This man we picking up today is one of those very good friends. He is an elderly man who lives in Nuna Lake. He broke his hip while visiting his daughter. We're bringing him home."

"That sounds like you: always doing something good. Did anyone ever tell you how much your Fresh Air Fund helps the city's kids? My wife works with children and says you have saved their backs many times."

Andy looked surprised. "I'm not sure what you're talking about."

"Your help in taking care of the kids who play in the park all summer. Most of them are pretty poor. Any time it rains your buses take all the kids somewhere – the museum, the movies – a gymnasium. It's really nice for you to provide transportation on those days so the kids can play safely out of the rain."

Joe paused for a moment and then said, "I believe we're almost there. I better get in my seat." He returned to the cockpit.

Sarah had sat quietly during their conversation. "You're a man of many surprises, Andy Mellon. And they all seem to be quite good. I've really worried about how much you spent on Hobie's phone. I guess I didn't need to worry."

The plane began to descend to land in Arizona.

Sarah had sat their so quietly it had Andy worried. Was she angry? Was she upset? Was she disappointed? He realized he liked Sarah. He liked her independent spirit, her good sense, but most of all, her compassion for other people. Would they still be friends?

They looked out the window as the plane landed and very quickly Sarah said, "There's Angela waiting for us." She waved to her friend.

"I can't believe you're doing all this for Dad," Angela said.

"It's Nuna Lake that's doing it," Andy said. "Nuna Lake is a special place." He hurried inside to greet his friend.

"Andy, it's you," Harry said as he saw his good friend.

"You bet it is and we're going to have you on that plane and on our way in fifteen minutes."

"I'll be so glad to get home. Does that place have a room for me or was it full?"

"Harry, you know I'd be on their backs if they didn't have room for you," Sarah said as she gave him a hug.

"Did you know, Sarah is my adopted daughter," he said with a smile. "Oh, I'm so glad to see you both. Can we leave for Nuna Lake right way?"

'I think we can. Let them be sure your bed is locked in tight and we'll be on our way."

"Dad, are you really sure this is what you want?" Angela asked her father.

"Angela, I love you. You are a good daughter. But I want to go home."

"Go with God, Daddy. I love you."

They secured his bed; Andy and Sarah fastened their seat belts and they were on their way to Nuna Lake.

Back in Nuna Lake an ambulance was waiting for Harry. They carried him from the plane. Sarah rode with Harry while Andy sent his plane back to New York. Then he drove his car to the convalescent center. Sarah was standing in the doorway of Harry's room smiling. The inside of Harry's room looked just like his room at home. His rocking chair was in the corner. A picture of his beloved Millie was on his nightstand. A bulletin board on his wall had pictures of his children and grandchildren. A big poster was on another wall filled with notes and cards from the town.

"I can't believe what this town has done for me," he said, nearly crying as he spoke.

"We love you, Harry. We're glad to have you home," Sarah said as she plumped his pillow and tucked his covers around him. "The mayor and everyone else want to come see you but decided to let you rest tonight. Tomorrow, get ready for lots of company."

His doctor arrived then so everyone left the room, telling him they would see him tomorrow. He asked Sarah and Mike to come to his bedside. He placed one hand in Andy's and one in Sarah's hand. "You are two of the most special people I have ever known. Thank you, thank you, thank you."

Andy and Sarah walked from the room together.

"Andy, thank you so much for what you did today. Harry is much weaker than I thought he would be. You made the trip so easy for him. How can we ever thank you?"

"Forgive me for not telling the truth about who I am. Somehow, I've been almost blaming the money for my lonely life. I had money but I didn't spend it because I turned from people who might have helped me. I've lived a lonely life. When I saw Harry's room restored for him I realized that money is not that important."

"But your money got him home. And your money helped heal Hobie."

"No, the town healed Hobie but my money helped."

They were quiet for a moment standing outside the car. Then he quietly asked, "Would you like to have dinner before going home?"

"If you'll settle for leftover lasagna, I have some in the fridge."

"I'd like that. Then I'll do the dishes and you can go to bed. It's been a long day." He paused. "We really didn't get time to talk about my confession of who I am…"

"I know who you are. A kind decent man. Let's go home."

Chapter 14

Andy thought Nuna Lake was a special place in the summer with flowers blooming everywhere, but nothing had prepared him for the gorgeous colors of autumn. It seemed that every tree was its own beautiful shade: red, purple; yellow, orange, even green and all shades in between. Andy wanted to put his arms around them and capture their beauty. The chrysanthemums were magnificent. Things were going well for him. If anyone who did know the secret of who he was, and told another, he did not know it. He was very glad to have Harry back in town. He stopped every night after work to see Harry, who seemed to be recovering very nicely. Even Hobie, whom Andy saw quite often, was special to Andy.

He continued to work in the lab under the careful eye of Martha, who now was back at work part time.

As for Sarah, they began to have dinner at least once a week or maybe twice. Her shop was so interesting. It was so neatly arranged that it took time to see everything in it. Her gift items were always classic. Julia, who worked for her was a dear, always suggesting that Sarah take time off for lunch when Andy stopped by.

When Andy walked down the street, strangers called him by name. Many old-timers in town wanted to buy him coffee to say thank you for his help in getting Harry home. Andy began to believe he could live in this town forever. If anyone guessed he was the benefactor putting large bills in the donation jars, no one talked about it. Even at work no mention was ever made of his past life. Andy began to realize that it was not his money that had made him a recluse, it was he, himself. Now he felt a little freer to offer help to someone in need.

He continued to live in Harry's house. Sometimes he got lonely there as he remembered how he and Harry had done things together, but he knew Harry was getting good care and might never return to his home. He thought a little about offering to buy Harry's house, but knew Harry still called it home. Harry's two children had come back from overseas to visit Harry and were very kind to Andy about looking after Harry.

Harry's hip was healing nicely. But, they wouldn't let him get out of bed without help and they wouldn't let him send out for food and they wouldn't let him have his TV turned up full blast. He could not go to the game room to play chess or checkers. They didn't put enough salt in his food. They insisted on changing his sheets every day. *Well,* he thought, *I asked to come here. In fact I insisted on it. I know it's the best place for me. But I'm missing everyday life. I want to go to the diner for chili. I want to see Joe at the newsstand. I want to see my Millie and hold her hand, and cuddle with her in our bed. I want….*

The nurse came by. "Anything I can get you?" she asked.

"I feel sorry for me," he told her.

"Really," she asked. "Why? Is there something we should be doing for you?"

"No, you're really quite nice. But I want to be in the house I shared with my Millie. I want to see the Hardware Store I owned for so many years…I want…"

Harry stopped talking and looked at the woman who was trying to help him. "I guess I'm having a pity party for me. I know this is the best place for me to be. Everyone is very kind. I guess I just got…well, you know."

"Harry, you have been a fixture in this town all my life. You and Millie were the kindest people in town. Maybe it's Millie you're missing today. I know you have her picture on your nightstand, but do you have something little you can hold when you think of her?"

"Millie had a shoebox of special mementos she treasured. Maybe if I had them to look at I'd feel better."

"Why don't I call Andy and ask him to look for the box? He could bring it to you tonight."

"I think I'd like that."

Andy got the phone call from the nurse and found the box of mementos to take to Harry. When he arrived with the box, Harry's eyes filled with tears as he saw how carefully Millie had saved them for him: her dance card from their high school prom, a letter he had written to her while he was in the service, the ring box from her engagement ring, the baptism dress all three children wore, well, the list went on and on. He held each one close to his face. It was almost like he could smell Millie's perfume on them – Chanel #5. He remembered how she treasured every thing in the box. She said it was like having a visit with the children. Well, today, for Harry it was like having a visit with Millie. Andy had thoughtfully left the room while Harry looked at his treasures, but soon went back in and let Harry show him each item and talk about them. Then Harry spoke.

"Do you have a box of treasures tucked away somewhere?" he asked Andy.

"Probably not, though I do remember my grandmother gave me a box. I'm not sure where it is anymore. Probably back in the penthouse."

Harry may have been old but his mind was sharp. "The penthouse? You lived in a penthouse?"

"Yeah, I guess I did." He paused looking down at his feet. Then he looked Harry in the eyes and asked, "Are you too tired to hear about me?"

"Never too tired for you, Andy."

"You might not like me when I'm done for I've been living a lie."

"Sit down and tell me."

Andy told Harry about his past life.

When he finished Harry said, "Then it was your plane that brought me home. You are a good man, Andy Mellon. I had heard rumors about it. The gossip all came from the airport when someone heard one of the pilots talking about 'your plane'".

Andy said nothing for a few minutes and then said, "It's only been lately that I could talk about my past. I was rich but lonely. I came to Nuna Lake and found friends, real friends. But I did live a lie, not letting anyone know the real truth."

"Did you tell a lie or just let people think what they wanted? That's not a lie."

"Harry, are you trying to make me feel good?"

"Yes, I am. Do you feel better now?"

"Yes. But it was something I didn't want to talk about."

"Then I did good." Harry paused and then continued. "You may have let us all think whatever we wanted to, but when we needed you, you were there for us. People were talking about all the big bills in the collection jar. But you supported the town with more than your money. You gave this town your time, your support, your energy…"

"Harry, I did what anyone would have done."

"Not so, not so. Some men would have done nothing. You gave of yourself sitting with Hobie all those hours. That's the kind of thing people remember. How you gave of yourself."

"Sorry, Andy," the nurse spoke coming into the room. "Harry's got another therapy session before bedtime. You'll need to come back tomorrow."

Chapter 15

Harry lay in his bed the next morning thinking. What could he do for Andy and Sarah? They had done so much for him. But what could he do? He realized he loved them both. Sarah had always been like a daughter to him and after living with Andy for the past months, Andy was like a son. They are two nice people. They've both been hurt with romance. But they both recovered. They need each other, he thought, but they're both proud, stubborn people. He'd have to think on this. The next couple of days, he did just that – think! He knew Sarah better than he knew Andy and if she thought he was meddling in her life, the whole plan would end right then. He needed to be subtle. He thought of this and that but he knew Sarah would see through any of his ideas. And she would get her hankers up and refuse to be a part of it. What could he do? And then he had an idea. The most romantic place in Nuna Lake was the Lake House. It was a fine dining place that had been written up in the gourmet magazines. Dorothy and Ed, the couple who owned it, were wonderful people and good friends of Harry. He gave them a call.

"Help," he said. "I want to play cupid for two nice people and I don't know how to do it. Can you help me?"

"Of course," Dorothy said. "We've had more romances start here than I can count. Who do you have in mind?"

'Sarah and Andy."

"I know Sarah well, but haven't met Andy yet. She's so good to everyone. Is he good enough for her," she asked.

"Andy is worthy. He came to town about six months or so and after a very quiet start, is now known by everyone. He and Sarah see each other all the time but only as good friends. I want to light a fire under them both."

"I think Sarah needs to remember she is a woman. She dresses in jeans all the time, usually has her hair in a pony tail and she rarely wears make up. She's a very successful business woman. We all love her but she doesn't elude romance since she broke up with the jerk. She's good friends with Rose. Maybe Rose will have an idea. I'm good friends with Julia, who works for Sarah. Should I ask her for ideas? If you can get them here for dinner, I can serve them a romantic dinner they won't forget."

"Anything you do is on my bill. Do you understand?" asked Harry.

"We'll see," she said with a smile.

Well, that's a start, he thought. He sat quietly thinking for a few minutes. Then he began to smile. Sarah's two best friends are Julia, who works for her, and Rose. "I'll call Rose."

"Rose, can you possibly come to see me today?" he asked very quietly.

"Of course, Harry. Is something wrong?" she asked.

"Yes, but I think you can fix it." He spoke very softly and slowly.

"I'll be right there."

"Okay," he answered slowly in what he hoped was a weak voice so she would hurry. He had to get this show on the road.

He laid back down and got under the covers. He wanted to make this look, well, look urgent.

"Why don't you close the door?" he asked very slowly and quietly when she came in.

"Of course."

"Can you pull a chair over by my bed?"

"Of course. Are you okay, Harry? You sound a bit down."

"I'm fine," he said popping up in bed. "But we have a problem and I've been lying here thinking about how to solve it. But I need your help."

"Of course. I'll be glad to help if I can. Tell me about it," she said as she sat down in the chair.

"It has to be kept very private. Understood?"

"Harry, what's going on? You have me concerned."

"We have to move Andy and Sarah beyond the friendship stage."

"What? What did you say?"

"You and I have to figure out a way to get Andy and Sarah beyond the friendship stage."

"Harry, you old romantic. You made me rush down here for this?"

"This is important. You know how I love Sarah. She's like a daughter to me. But that scumbag she had around for years made her forget about love in her life. Andy is a fine man who will take good care of her. He may have come to Nuna

Lake as a mystery man but he didn't run away when we had trouble. He was here to help anyone he could. I do believe he is a fine man. But both of them were hurt by past romances and are afraid to reach out for each other. Did you ever really look at them together? They are like an old married couple but I doubt he's ever kissed her. Here's how I think we can help them.

"They will have dinner at the Lake House. They will be dressed up and look beautiful and handsome. Then Dorothy will serve them a romantic dinner and they will recognize that they love each other."

Rose started to laugh. "I swear, Harry, you are the most romantic person I know."

"Everyone falls in love at the Lake House. Didn't you and Mike begin your romance there?"

"That was different."

"Of course it wasn't. But we have to make this romance happen. I already called Dorothy and she's going to help us."

"You what? You called Dorothy?"

"Yes. She's an old friend and thinks we should do it tonight."

"Tonight? Harry, I think you have too much time on your hands."

Harry ignored Rose's outcries. "This is how I think it will work. You and Mike invite them both to go with you to the Lake House. You plan to meet them there. Andy and Sarah arrive and get a message from you and Mike that something came up and you cannot be there. Dorothy serves them a romantic dinner. They realize they love and need each other. Job done!"

"Harry, I'll say it again. You have too much time on your hands."

"It will work. I know it will work. If we don't push them a little they'll be a hundred-year-old couple who are only friends. We have to make this happen."

"Harry, you know how Sarah hates to dress up."

"And you know just how to get her in a new dress for dinner."

Rose sat quietly. "I'm not sure this will work. You know how stubborn Sarah can be. I love her and don't want to lose her friendship."

"I know you want her to be happy. She has many, many friends, but few real friends that care about her. She needs a little nudge from you. She loves you and trusts you. And she will say thank you to you when it's over. I know Sarah like one of my own daughters. She deserves someone who will be good to her. I used to think there would be no one in Nuna Lake good enough to heal her heart. I'm sure Andy has done that. But they are like two old folks with each other. We need to wake them both up. When Andy sees her all dressed up he'll know she's the one for him. And Andy needs her. When he came to Nuna Lake I pegged him as a very lonely man. He made friends so quietly no one saw it. But he's a good man who quietly steps in to take care of things. He will take good care of Sarah."

Rose sat quietly for a few minutes. "I'll have to talk to Mike about it first, but I guess I could help Sarah shop for a dress."

"Okay, you can go now, Rose, and talk to Mike. And I can take a little nap and rest easy. This will work, you'll see."

Rose made her way to her car and sat quietly. She had to admit she hoped Harry's scheme would work but... She reached for her phone and called Mike.

"I need to talk with you. Can you get away for a quick lunch?" she asked him.

"I got a meeting at one o'clock. Is something wrong?"

"I'll talk fast. See you at the diner in fifteen minutes."

She drove immediately there. *Harry is so right about getting Sarah and Andy together, but should anyone interfere,* she wondered?

Mike practically pulled in the parking lot behind her.

"What's wrong?" he asked.

"Harry wants me to be a buttinsky."

"What?"

"Harry thinks Sarah and Andy need to be given a shove so they can fall in love."

"I think Harry's right."

"What?"

"Oh, come on now. You have seen them together. They're like an old married couple."

"Really, Mike. Do you really think so?"

"I've been surprised you and your gal pals haven't pushed the romance along."

"Mike Nelson. You shock me. You always say everyone should mind their own business."

"Those two need a shove. Have you seen them together lately? I repeat. They're like an old married couple."

"It may interest you to know that Harry wants you to be a part of the scheme."

"What do I have to do?"

"Invite Andy to have dinner at the Lake House. Then we phone the Lake House and tell them we can't make it. They will be left alone to have a romantic dinner."

"What a great plan. Was it your idea or Harry's?"

"Harry's idea. But he already called Dorothy at the Lake House and she's setting up the plan."

"Don't know why we didn't think of it. Didn't we fall in love at the Lake House? It's where I kissed you for the first time. Remember that?" he said touching her cheek.

"Yes, I do remember. I remember how happy I was that night." Rose said quietly.

"It's the right thing to do. Sarah and Andy have had no romance for so long they've forgotten how it works. If it's meant to be, it will be. A little shove from us won't hurt."

"Oh, Mike, I don't want Sarah to get hurt."

"And I don't want Andy to get hurt, Rose. They're both strong people. One night of matchmaking isn't going to ruin their lives. They may see through this whole scheme and have a good laugh over it."

"Maybe you're right."

She sat with her coffee for a few minutes then headed for Sarah's Card and Gift Shop.

Sarah and Julia were unpacking a new shipment of gifts.

"Sarah, I hope you're free tonight. Mike and I would like to take you and Andy to dinner at the Lake House. I know your store is open tonight but you can take off one night can't you?"

"Of course she can. My husband is out of town so I can close the store," Julia said.

"Rose, you're very nice but why go to the Lake House? Let's eat at the diner."

"No where to talk there. Mike is going to ask Andy. He's been worried about how to thank him for his help with Harry. I don't want to be the only woman there, so I decided to ask you. The men will probably talk roses all night."

"Rose, you're one of the nicest people I know but the Lake House is too fancy."

"You're just saying that because you hate wearing a dress unless it's down to your ankles," Julia said.

"Well, actually, I'm sick of all my clothes," Rose said. "I'm going to the dress shop when I leave here. I hope I can find something new to wear."

Julia spoke up. "Go with her, Sarah. You haven't had any thing new for ages."

"Oh, I don't know. I don't want to disappoint you, Rose. You've been so good to me. But the Lake House....a new dress...I wouldn't know how to act."

"That's ridiculous, you'll be yourself," Rose answered. "Come on, let's go. You can finish unpacking that box later."

"Well, maybe it wouldn't hurt to look," Sarah said.

"Let's go," Rose said before Sarah could change her mind. Once in the store, Sarah was a bit over-whelmed.

"I don't think they have my size here."

"Good afternoon, Sarah," said Martha the shop owner. "How's business?"

They exchanged chitchat, Rose browsed the store not seeing anything she thought might be appropriate and Sarah would like. This would not be easy. She pulled out two dresses.

"Why not try on these dresses?" she asked Sarah.

"Well, I guess I could," Sarah answered somewhat reluctantly.

The dresses were not suitable at all. Rose began to be discouraged for she could see Sarah just didn't like them.

Then Martha said, "I have a dozen new dresses in the back room that I haven't put out yet. Now that I know what you like and dislike, let me go and get them."

She came back with two of the dresses. One was a shiny gray silk with no sleeves, a deep-V neckline and about ankle length. Sarah refused to even try it on. The other dress was the proverbial 'little black dress.'

"Would you call that a funeral dress?" Sarah said with a smile.

"It will be your funeral dress if you don't try it on," Rose said.

When Sarah came out of the dressing room she was transformed. The dress fit her perfectly. It was made of soft black crepe. It had a short V-neck, long fitted sleeves and a small flare to the skirt. It fit her perfectly. Martha had stepped out of her own black heels and gave them to Sarah so she could see the whole effect.

Rose had seen Sarah dressed up before, but never anything like this. She glowed with beauty.

"Oh, my. Oh, my," Rose was almost speechless. "Oh, how beautiful you look. So classy. You look like a runway model."

Sarah said nothing. She just kept looking at herself in the mirror. "I haven't felt this good in...I can't even remember the last time." She stood there quietly looking at herself in the mirror. Then she spoke quietly. "When I was with...

you know… he told me I looked like Morticia Adams of the Adams family. I haven't worn black since then."

Martha, the saleswoman said, "A simple gold chain and a pair of gold earrings would accent your face beautifully."

Sarah spoke softly. "I have those pieces. They belonged to my grandmother."

Rose spoke. "Sarah, you're a beautiful, beautiful woman. I always knew you were beautiful on the inside. But in that dress you are a confident, beautiful woman who could take on the world."

"Maybe I do need to dress up more and be concerned about how I look." She kept looking at herself and she turned slowly to see all angles. "I have forgotten how the proper clothes can change how you feel. I need to buy some shoes, though. I'm sure there is nothing in my closet to go with this dress."

"I carry a small line of designer shoes here in the shop. Let me see what I have in your size," Martha said.

Sarah kept turning around looking at herself.

"Rose," she said quietly. "Thank you for making me come here. I have remembered too long all the hateful things he said that hurt me so much and made me feel inferior. I am a good business woman. I need to remember that and dress accordingly. I need to dress appropriately. I need to do something to my hair. I need…"

"Slow down, Sarah," Rose said coming to put her arms around the woman. "The clothes you wear, the style of your hair doesn't change who you are. You are one of the kindest, sweetest women I know. Whether you're in your jeans or this beautiful dress, you are still the same, wonderful Sarah."

Martha did find shoes that fit Sarah and Sarah left the shop, promising to come back later for a whole new wardrobe. But she was quiet and pensive as they walked to the car.

"Rose, do you think your hairdresser could fit me in this afternoon. I need to do something with my hair."

Rose was so happy she felt like crying. "I have an appointment at four o'clock. You take my appointment."

Rose could hardly wait to tell Mike about her successful afternoon. "Mike, you can't believe how beautiful she really is," she kept saying.

"Well, maybe I'd better tell you about my day. While you were busy with Sarah, I was busy with Andy. He insisted he wanted to take us for dinner. But then he thought about his clothes."

"Is the Lake House a formal dining room?" Andy had asked

"I told him the men usually have a tie and/or a jacket. He said he only had casual clothes in Nuna Lake so I offered to lend him a jacket, but he wouldn't let me. He said he would go buy something. So I gave him the rest of the afternoon off. I got to hand it to Harry. He knows people better than anyone else."

It had been a long time since Andy had bought any clothes. He was surprised to see that lapels on men's jackets had changed over the years. And such bright colors. Even the ties looked different. *I bet my closet in New York is full of clothes that are terribly out of style now,* he thought. He was fortunate that he was a strict size forty, and he found a shirt, slacks, jacket and tie. They didn't quite fit him like his tailored suits did, but as he looked in the mirror, he thought he looked dapper. He was feeling good.

He decided to call Sarah. No sense in both of them driving to the Lake House. He reached for his phone.

"I guess you know we're invited out to dinner with Rose and Mike."

"I heard about that, too," Sarah answered him.

"Want to share a ride? I can pick you up around seven."

"Yes."

"Is there anything wrong? You sound a bit subdued. Had a bad day?"

"No, it's not that. It's just that…well, I don't go to the Lake House much. I think the last time I was there was for Mike and Rose's wedding. It is really nice but I'll probably use the wrong soup spoon."

"Well, if they serve us soup, I'll drink it from my bowl. See you in twenty minutes."

"Okay."

Being dressed up felt sort of strange to Andy. He certainly didn't want his limo to take Sarah to the Lake House, but his car was terribly old and a bit out of style. *Because I am dressed up, does that make this a real date? No, it is not a date. Sarah is Sarah. Certainly she is the best friend I have in Nuna Lake. But, not the only friend. Those guys at work: I know about their wives and children or their girl friends.* He thought of Judy, Hobie and Katie. He could stop by their house any time and be welcomed in. Gabe was becoming like a brother to him. And how could he forget Harry? He knew he could talk to Rose or Mike about anything.

He pulled into Sarah's driveway. Somehow, having a tie on made him remember his manners. Honking the horn to let her know he was there seemed sort of juvenile. He got out of the car and went to the door.

She opened the door. For a second he couldn't believe his eyes. He expected to see Sarah dressed up a little, but who is this goddess standing in Sarah's doorway? She was beautiful beyond any words he knew. "Sarah, is it really you?" he asked in a quivering voice.

"It's me," she answered quietly.

"You look beautiful. Your hair…your ponytail is gone. You have gorgeous hair."

"You mean I cleaned up okay?" she asked. "I had highlights put in my hair. You're looking good yourself. I've never seen you wear anything but jeans."

"The slacks and jacket are new. I heard the Lake House is a pretty fancy place. I didn't think jeans were acceptable."

"Well, the dress is new, too. I realized I hadn't bought a dress for years. Rose helped me choose it. Do you approve?"

"Oh yeah, oh yeah. You look good."

They both were quiet on the ride to the restaurant.

Dorothy greeted them when they arrived. She introduced herself to Andy, told Sarah she looked beautiful and showed them to their table. It was by the window that looked out on the lake. The reflections of the multicolored trees around the lake was magnificent. They were seated with their backs to the room so they could enjoy the view.

Dorothy brought them a small plate with tiny appetizers on it as she poured them a glass of wine. "This is a new appetizer we may add to our menu. Let me know what you think. I do have some news for you. We just had a call from Mike. I'm sorry to tell you that Rose and Mike will not be joining you. Something came up; they hope you will understand; they will talk with you later. Here's today's menu."

"I hope everything is okay with Rose and Mike," Sarah said. "They are two really, really special people."

"Sarah, I'm getting a funny feeling."

"Are you sick?"

"No, no, nothing like that."

"What do you mean?"

"Do you think someone is setting us up?"

"What? What do you mean?"

"Do you find it unusual that Mike and Rose are not here?"

"Yes, it is unusual. They're really particular about everything."

"I think they wanted us to have an evening away from the hustle and bustle of every day life," Andy said.

Sarah sat quietly. "You could be right. Rose had me out the door of my shop and to the dress shop in no time at all."

"If she did, I'm glad she did it."

"You are?"

"You look like a goddess tonight."

"You'll make me blush," she said.

About seven courses of food later, Andy said, "I can't even look at any more food."

"Me, neither," Sarah answered.

They sat quietly looking out the window. An early sprinkle of snow had begun to fall. The lake, the lights, the trees and bushes and the sparkle of the light snow made the area look like a fairyland.

"Isn't it beautiful out there?" Sarah spoke quietly.

"Nuna Lake is beautiful. I never expected to find anywhere like this when I left New York."

"Do you miss the city?"

"No, I don't miss it. But I let no one know where I was going. I know now how morose and unhappy I was. I skipped town without telling anyone."

"You must have had some friends there."

"Very few. He was quiet for a few minutes. "Well, maybe we should leave. Could I have our check, please?" he asked a passing waiter.

Dorothy came to the table. "Your dinner tonight is with the compliments of a benefactor. The bill has been paid."

"That sounds like Mike - always thinking ahead."

"It was not Mike and Rose who paid for your dinner."

"Then who?"

"He wishes to remain anonymous. Ed and I were disappointed that we didn't think of this first for we owe you so much for the help you gave the town when Tom died and Hobie was so ill. And bringing Harry home. But we hope you will accept this gift certificate from Ed and me and come back again."

"Not Dorothy and Ed. Not Mike and Rose. Who do you think could have set this up?" Andy asked Sarah.

"I think I know," Sarah said with a smile. "Stop and think for a minute. Who is the one person who is constantly meddling in our lives?"

Together they both said, "Harry."

"He's considers himself the Nuna Lake matchmaker," Sarah said.

"Well, he never stops singing praises about you to me. He tells me you're his other daughter. He's playing matchmaker."

"And he constantly tells me what a good man you are. What time is it?" she asked.

"Just after ten."

"He always listens to the ten o-clock news. Let's call him," she said reaching for her phone and pressing the speaker button.

"Harry, you'll never guess what just happened. I'm with Andy and we have just had the most delightful dinner at the Lake House."

"Oh, really. I hear they have good food there."

"You'll never guess what else happened. Some benefactor paid our bill. Can you imagine anyone doing that?"

"I guess someone likes you," Harry answered.

"And I guess that 'someone' had better know how much we both appreciate the fine dinner."

"I'm getting very tired now so I'll talk with you later," Harry said in a fake 'tired' voice.

"You can't fool me, Harry." Sarah said. "This was a set up to get me in a dress."

"Did it work?"

"She's the most beautiful woman I've ever seen," Andy said.

"I have to hang up now. I'm very tired," he repeated. "You will see that she gets home okay, won't you?" he asked in the fake old voice.

"Not only do I see how beautiful she is, I see what a schemer you are."

"Not me," Harry said. "Not me."

"Goodnight, Harry," they both said together.

Harry could not wait to get off the line. He had two important calls to make – one to Dorothy to say thank you and the other to Mike and Rose to let them know his plan had worked.

Andy drove carefully on the roads which were becoming slick, When they got to Sarah's he got out of the car to walk her to the door. She slipped on a slippery spot and Andy reached out to catch her. He pulled her close to him. She looked at him. There, by the car, they stood and kissed. Sarah quietly said, "Wow, you sure know how to kiss a girl."

"I need practice," Andy said and kissed her again.

They slowly made their way to her front door.

"Can we do this again?" Andy asked her.

"I'd like that," she answered very quietly.

As she put her key in the lock, Andy spoke. "Sarah, this has been one of the best evenings of my life. You are a beautiful, beautiful woman. Every man in that restaurant tonight envied me."

Sarah spoke "It has been a special night. One I'll never forget. You are a very special man, Andy. Instead of being angry with Harry..."

Andy interrupted "I need to thank Harry. I should have thought this up myself. Can I call you tomorrow?"

"I'd like that."

They kissed one more time. Then Sarah went inside her door and Andy returned to his car and got in. But almost like magic, Andy got out of his car and returned to the front door just as Sarah opened it. They embraced one more time and moved inside her house.

Chapter 16

The next morning Andy awoke feeling wonderful. He couldn't remember ever feeling this way before. He felt content. He felt happy. He felt….well, he couldn't even describe it. He felt glad to be alive. When had he ever felt this way in his life? By the time he had coffee, the old feelings began to descend on him. But this time, he felt them coming and knew what they were. It was the feelings of living a double life – part Nuna Lake (the wonderful part) – part New York (the lonely part). Should he continue to live this way – or was it time to make a decision about the rest of his life? He thought about Sarah – how it felt to have her in his arms – how it felt to make love to her. He had always thought there would never be another woman in his life. He hadn't even missed Gretchen when she left. He was glad she was gone. But how would he feel if Sarah was not in his life? In spite of what he heard about her old boyfriend, she must have loved him. If he came back today would she welcome him back? Could he survive it? He paced the floor until he knew Sarah would be up. He dialed her number.

"Good morning, Andy."

"Did anyone ever tell you that you have a very pleasant voice?" he asked.

"No, but thank you. You sound good, too."

They were quiet for a moment. Then the both started to speak. Laughing, Sarah said, "You go first."

"I just wondered what your plans were for today," he asked.

"I plan to change around a lot of things in the store to get ready for Christmas. I've got four high-school kids coming to work today. The two girls will run the front of the store and the two guys are going to help me move boxes and counters. Christmas is always a big season here. Did you hear about the parade on the Saturday after Thanksgiving? Hobie was asked to be the Grand Marshall. That means he sits on top of the leading convertible. His mom and Katy will be in the car. The next car will have the parents of the two teen boys who died in the accident. I hope the bad weather holds off a bit longer."

"Sounds like Nuna Lake really celebrate the holidays. Do you need extra help getting ready? I could stop by around lunch time. I want to go out to the lab this morning and check on the rose bushes. We tried a new treatment on one yesterday and I have to check it out."

"That would be great. Call me before you come. I may have you pick up some lunch for us all."

"Will do. I'll give you a call."

Andy had a smile on his face as he hung up the phone. He headed for the nursery. Mike had given him keys to the place for he often wanted to check on some plant during the weekend. He was a little disturbed that the treatment he had tried didn't work. It was one he had used on his bushes back in New York. He stopped for a moment to think about New York. Was it time for him to decide about where he wanted to make his permanent home? Why does he want to hold on to his penthouse if he doesn't live there? With many questions in his mind he made his way to the lab. He was surprised to see Mike's truck in the parking lot.

"Anyone home?" he called out as he made his way to the lab.

"Hi, Andy, what brings you here today?" he heard Mike ask.

"Probably the same thing as you. How do the roses look today?"

"I don't think the treatment we tried is working."

Andy made his way to the roses and took a long look at them, shaking his head. "Not quite as good as yesterday. I wonder what's wrong. Do they need more or less of the treatment we gave them yesterday?"

"I really don't have any idea," Mike said. "I'd really, really hate to lose them."

"I know who can tell us what's wrong," Andy said. "Marvin Hartley."

"I'm sure Marvin Hartley would know," Mike said. "But I have never met the man. I can't very well ask him for help."

Andy smiled. "I can. He's the man taking care of my roses at the penthouse. I haven't seen or talked with him for six months or so but I know he continues to care for my roses each week. He might desert everything else but he would never desert the roses. I'll give him a call."

Andy dialed his number.

"Marvin Hartley here," the voice said.

"Andy Mellon here," he said. "How are you Marv?"

"Andrew! Andrew! Is it really you? It's been months Is it really you?"

"It's really me, Marv."

"Where are you? Are you okay? What happened to you? Oh, it's so good to hear from you. I've missed you."

"Marv, it's a long story. I guess you might say I was on a quest to get a life. And I did. Hearing your strong, steady voice helps me to know what I need to do. I need to end my double life. My new life brought me to Nuna Lake. Actually, that's why I'm calling you. I ended up working for Mike Nelson, who has a landscaping, greenhouse, well, the works. He is also working on the new grass we heard about."

"I've heard his name but I've never met him."

"You both have the same work ethic about your plants. Actually that's why I'm calling. "We need your opinion about treatment on a rose bush. I recommended the same thing we used on our roses but it didn't work. We need your expert advice. We'd like to save the rose."

Marv asked several questions about the plant.

"It's hard for me to say, being so far away." The phone was quiet for a minute. Then he said, "Where is Nuna Lake? Could I get there and back home the same day? My wife has been ill and I don't want to be away overnight, but I'd like to see your plants."

"I'm sorry to hear your wife is ill. But I could easily fly you here to see the plant if you could come."

"Do you think we could do it right away? Actually, I was going to call your Business Manager to try to reach you. I'm closing my business to spend time with my wife. She has been so ill I decided it was time to sell the business. But we can talk about that when I see you."

"I'm so sorry to hear about that. But you're right. We should do it immediately. Is tomorrow a good day for you? I still have my plane which is always on standby. If they bring you in the morning we can have you home before bedtime."

"Let's do it."

"Marv, it will be really good to see you. You and Mima are the only persons I missed when I left New York. I'll make the arrangements right away." He hung up the phone and said to Mike, "I guess you heard all that. He'll be here tomorrow. He's closing his business because his wife is ill." Andy paused and sat quietly for a minute. Then he turned to Mike and repeated, "He's the person I really missed when I left New York." He sat quietly for a minute or so.

Mike just sat there quietly and then said, "Marvin Hartley is one of the really great men when it comes to roses. And he's coming here......" He shook his head. "I feel so honored."

"He's one of the nicest men I know. I left many acquaintances in New York, but only one real friend – Marvin." Andy stood there quietly, shaking his head.

"Wait till I tell Gabe who came here." Mike said.

"Why not ask Gabe to be here tomorrow? You call Gabe. I'll call the airport."

After he made arrangements for his plane to bring Marvin to Nuna Lake, Andy looked at his watch. It was nearly twelve o'clock. He had promised to take lunch to Sara. He immediately called her.

"I'm so sorry I'm late. I got tied up in business. I'm on my way now."

"Great. I just called and ordered pizza. I ordered enough for you too. Can you pick it up?"

"Of course. See you later." He turned to Mike and said, "I'm sorry, Mike, I'll call you about the plane times. Got to run."

Mike just smiled and said, "Call me."

The pizza was ready when Andy got there. He hurried to the shop where they were waiting. Sarah told the young people to eat while she worked the store. Andy decided to wait and eat with Sarah. He was surprised at the new look as counters were moved.

"No wonder you're successful. You keep a new look to the place," he told her. "And it doesn't hurt business that you're so beautiful," he said.

"My, oh my," she said. "You must have had a very successful morning."

"Let me tell you the high points." He told her what was happening with Marvin. Then he quietly said. "I'm finally letting go of what my life used to be. It was an existence, not a life. But tell me what you're doing here."

"A couple of years ago, Rose's mother put me in contact with an international group out of London. They travel a lot to Africa. They buy local crafts that the people make. I contacted them and said I had a shop and I'd like to help them. Their one big concern was that I might want to make money on the things. With this group 100% of the money goes back to the town's people. I assured them I'd do this. My contribution is that I buy the merchandise from them at a cheap price. When I moved from next door into this shop I set up this one section that always has some ware that is one-of-a-kind. Since nothing is mass produced, everything is unique. This town has really responded to it. But I do like to put it front and center during the holidays."

"Did anyone ever tell you what a good person you are?" he asked.

"I think I heard that once before," she laughed.

Mike was very excited as he drove home. The great Marvin Hartley was coming to Nuna Lake. And he was going to look at Mike's roses. He felt like a little kid. He could hardly wait to tell Rose all about it. As they ate their lunch he told her all about the upcoming visit.

"I have an idea," Rose said. "It's going to be a very long day for Marvin. Why don't you bring everyone back here for lunch?"

"Rose, that's a wonderful idea. Could you expand the food to include the pilot who is going to fly him here? I think I heard he wants to talk with Andy. Oh, yes, I do have some gossip for you. Guess who had to leave the greenhouse quickly because he had to pick up lunch for a certain shopkeeper in Nuna Lake?"

"Oh, Mike. That's so exciting. I just know those two are made for each other. Maybe I'll ask Sarah to help me tomorrow."

The plane left New York at seven and was due to arrive in Nuna Lake a little after nine. Andy waited in his little old car. He wondered what Marv would think. *I doubt he'll even notice,* he thought. Marv's mind was always on his flowers. *It's funny, I was just wondering if it was time to cut all my New York ties and then this happens.* It was nice to know he had a plane at his disposal. It was nice to have access to someone who really knows roses and be able to call on them. Even his pilots. He had two of them, Joe and Hank. One or the other was always available. He knew that his money helped make this all possible. He liked and trusted his broker. He liked and trusted his business manager. Could he keep his plane? Did he want to keep his penthouse? He had already decided his wardrobe had to go. His old clothes no longer fit him. His weight had stayed the same but his flab had turned to muscle. He sat and thought about his old life, both the good and bad things that had happened. Then he saw the plane landing. He went toward it to greet his old friend.

"Marv, it's just wonderful to see you. I'm so sorry your wife is ill. But I'm glad you could get away today."

"Andrew, Andrew, it's so good to see you after all these months. You look just wonderful," Marv said. "And such luxury. Your limo came to my house to bring me to the airport. I had the whole plane to myself. The pilot asked me if I wanted to sit up front with him. It was an exciting trip."

"I'm afraid I have no limo to drive you. Only my little old Ford."

"Andrew, you look so healthy."

"Life in Nuna Lake is very different but very rewarding. I ran away from New York. I left everything behind. I bought an old car, some old clothes at the Salvation Army and started off. I had seen pictures of some beautiful gardens that I decided

I should see. They were and are magnificent. I told them my name was Andy Mellon. Only a very few people here know who I really am. Mike is one of them. Gabe is another. He works for Mike. He is most anxious to meet you. They both are. They have heard of your work with roses."

"I've worked in this field for over sixty years and loved every minute of it. But my wife needs me and I know it's time to let it go. I put it up for sale. I have people interested in buying the property but no one wants the greenhouses or my plants. They say the lot is too small. Anyhow, I heard the area is being rezoned to be residential only."

"Whoever buys it had better take good care of it," Andy said. "Here we are," he said as they pulled up in front of the building. It was Sunday and the parking lot was empty.

Mike came out of the building immediately. "Hello, I'm Mike Nelson. Thank you for coming all this distance to look at my roses. I feel very honored to meet you," he added as they shook hands.

"Andrew has been so good to me over the years. I feel very flattered that he thinks enough of me to tell you he even knows me."

"Your reputation has spread all over the United States. You're the go-to man for anyone with a problem with roses. Let me show you our problem."

He led Marv into the section of the plant with the roses. Gabe and Andy followed behind.

Marv asked many questions about the care of the roses and was pleased that every thing that touched the roses had been recorded in a notebook. He brought along little tools which he used to measure the moisture and chemicals in the soil. After he had tested and measured everything he asked for time to sit and think.

He looked at the men sitting there quietly and then said "I know what's wrong. Now I have to think of a cure."

They continued to sit there quietly. From time to time he looked in his little book to check on something. Finally, he said, "I think you should space out the treatment you are using. You are using the right solution but I think you should water it down and give them treatment every two hours for twenty-four hours and then every four hours for forty-eight hours. Then you should be able to go back to regular treatments."

"Then you think they will survive?"

"They will produce beautiful roses for you next summer."

"Was the disease the same one I had on my roses last summer?" Andy asked.

"No, that was different. But I think what I am suggesting will work. It's good that you kept good records of what you had tried. Those are exactly what I would have suggested first. But I saw it hadn't worked this time."

"How can I ever thank you for coming here and helping us? When Andy told us he knew you, we were impressed, but to have you come here is a great honor," Mike told him.

Andy spoke. "Marv, I was very secretive about who I was when I came to Nuna Lake. I finally told Mike and Gabe about it after a time. I've only told a very few others. It's not that I'm trying to hide it here. I frankly don't think anyone here cares. But slowly I made friends in town. I'm not sure it would matter to anyone now."

"Are you happy here? Have you made real friends here?" he asked.

"I'm very happy here, Marv."

"My wife is preparing lunch for us at my home. I hope you will join us," Mike invited.

"That would be very nice. Didn't I read in a magazine about gardens you have restored? Will lunch be at that house? I would like very much to see them."

"That's the house but I'm afraid the flowers have gone."

"But the plants are there. They are beautiful even when they sleep."

Andy spoke. "Let's do this. "Mike, you and Gabe head for home with Marv. I'll pick up Joe, our pilot, at the airport and bring him to lunch. Does that sound like a plan?"

"Sounds good to me," Mike said. "Let's go now."

"I hear them call you Andy instead of Andrew." Marv said as they walked to the cars.

"Yes, I left Andrew Mellon in New York and became Andy Mellon when I got here. I became one of the town people. Some of them may know I have money. But Nuna Lake is very different from my circle of friends in New York. It doesn't matter to the people here, one way or the other. This is a very unique place to live. Everyone knows everyone else, yet in a way everyone is very private about their own business."

"You look happy, Andrew. You look content. Yet I sense a bit of hesitation in your life."

"Well, you're right. Before we realized we had a "rose emergency" yesterday, I had been wondering if it was time I sold my penthouse and cut my ties to New York. Or maybe it was time to go back and try to take what I've learned here back to the city."

"Andrew, were you happy in New York? You rarely left your penthouse. You were surrounded with riches, but always seemed to be a loner. Except for Mima, who was a dear, you seemed to have no friends. As I worked with you on your garden, I got to know the kind, gentle man you are. But you let no one else see it. You are a good man, Andrew Mellon. You deserve happiness."

"I know you must be having some days that are not so happy. Tell me about your wife. Has she been ill long?"

"She has been very ill and requires round-the-clock care. We have her at home and I have help come in. But I decided to sell my business. I have found a buyer. I was glad when you called because I wanted you to know I can no longer take care of your penthouse garden."

"What about the roses? The ones we were experimenting with; did you sell that part of your business?"

"Those were your rose bushes. They are yours to keep, sell, or do whatever you want to do."

"No, Marv, those roses are yours. You planted them, watered them, fertilized them, and watched them grow. I realized a while back that those are your rose bushes. Take them home, plant them and enjoy them. Put the roses in a vase for your wife to enjoy."

"I can't do that. You funded the whole project. The rose world would flip upside down if you don't report on them."

"My name should never have been mentioned in connection with the roses."

"You funded the project. It wouldn't have happened without your help."

"I can't really accept credit for that."

"You must."

They left the nursery: Mike, Gabe, and Marv in one car; Andy left to pick up Joe.

Rose met them at the door and welcomed Marv to their home.

"You have prepared such a beautiful table. Where did you find these little flowers at this time of the year?"

"Mike has a little garden in the back of one of his buildings that gets sun and heat all year round."

"Oh, now I really remember who you are. So you're "the" Mike Nelson and you're his wife. You were in a magazine once."

"I confess, I'm that Mike Nelson," he said with a smile.

"Do I have time to see the gardens?" he asked.

"We do. Let's go," said Mike.

Andy and Joe joined them a few minutes later and then Rose called them to lunch. Marv especially loved the chicken soup Rose had prepared.

"Andrew, do you have a moment for us to talk or do you want to visit with Marv?" Joe asked as they finished eating.

"Rose, can we have another cup of your good coffee while we talk?" Andy asked.

"Sit right over there. I'll bring you coffee."

"What's on your mind?" Andy asked Joe as they were seated.

"I know you've spent the past few months living in Nuna Lake. Do you come to New York often?"

"No, I haven't been back since I left a few months ago."

"Well, I know you haven't used your plane much."

"And, you wonder if I'm going to sell it. Is that what you are going to ask me?" Andy asked.

"Actually, no. But Hank and I were wondering if you plan to stay in Nuna Lake?"

Andy sat quietly for a minute and then said, "Honestly, I don't know how to answer you. I ran away from New York and have a new, good life here. I'm happy here." He paused and then said, "Why do you ask?"

"For more than a year now Hank and I have been planning to start our own business. We have been watching for an airfield to buy. When we came to fly you to Arizona a month or so ago, we found out that the airfield in Sprucedale is going to be up for sale. They have regular flights to and from Chicago each day and a few other flights during the week. It's a field we think we would like to buy. We've done some research. It appears that the big box companies like Fed-Ex and UPS are looking for a drop zone in this area. That would be a big contract and could even bring business to the area. We each own our own small plane and would like to offer flying lessons. We don't expect to bring the big planes into the area, but we are finding a market for smaller planes." He sat quietly for a minute. "I guess what I'm asking you is this: would you consider having your plane housed here instead of New York?"

"That never entered my mind." Andy sat there quietly. "I guess you take me by surprise. I never gave it any thought. But maybe I should. Are you looking for investment dollars?"

"We think we have enough saved to get started. We still have work to do, but knowing what you pay in New York to house your plane would give us a great start."

"Do you have a business plan developed?"

"Yes. We tried to think of everything."

Andy sat and thought for a couple of minutes. Then he asked, "Are the hangers here large enough for my plane?"

"Just barely. We've tried to plan for a couple of new and larger hangars."

"What about the licensing?"

"That will probably be our next step. We've been working on these plans for a couple of years now. We just couldn't find the right place to do it."

Andy looked up and saw Mike and Marv come into the room. He knew his talk with Joe needed to end. "Fax me a copy of your business plan. I'll have my business manager review it."

He paused for a minute and then said. "I think maybe your plan might be what I need to finally make a decision about my life." Then he asked, "Is it time for you to leave Nuna Lake?"

"Yes, I think we'd better leave. Your limo should be waiting for Marv in New York. I know he is anxious to get home to his wife."

"Thank you, for bringing him here. I know it's Sunday, and I shouldn't bother you, but it turned out to be a day his daughter can stay with her mother. And maybe he needed a break from taking care of her. I think he enjoyed his day."

Marv did enjoy the day. As Rose told him goodbye she gave him a container of the soup she had served at lunch for his wife, along with tiny cup cakes she had served for desert, and the little bouquets of flowers that decorated the table. "Give these to your wife along with my best wishes."

"You are a very gracious hostess and a wonderful cook. I will give them to her with your best wishes."

Andy left to return to the airport with Joe and Marv. "Nuna Lake has been very good to me," he said, "but I still have so many ties to New York. I think I have some hard decisions to make. Marv, I'll let you know about the roses on the terrace. I think it's time I make up my mind about New York. Joe, fax me that information as soon as you can."

Andy headed back home after leaving the airport. He thought about his life in Nuna Lake. *Well, certainly I am not ready to leave. I have Sarah to think about. She will never leave Nuna Lake. Do I want her in my life? Do I want to stay in Nuna Lake?* Her house was only a short distance away so he decided to stop by.

"Do you mind drop-in company?" he asked Sarah when she answered the door.

"I'm glad to see you. How did the visit with Marv go? Did he solve your problems?"

"Probably. He gave us a new treatment to try. I think it will work."

"Then the visit went well."

"Actually it was a day with news. But tell me about your day first. Did you get the shop back in order to open tomorrow?"

"Yes. Julia and I worked all day and if I do say so myself, it looks great."

"I should have been there to help you."

163

"That sounds nice - someone to help me," she said quietly, looking down at the floor. But she quickly recovered and asked, "Are you hungry? How about some coffee?"

"Are you hungry? Can I take you out for something?

"How about a burger? I'll toss some on the grill?"

"That is something I know how to cook," he told her. "Let me cook them."

Together they made their way to the kitchen. When they accidentally bumped into one another, they immediately reached for each other.

Chapter 17

When Andy awoke the next morning he didn't know where he was for a minute. Then he saw he was not home. He remembered Sarah; making love with her, feeling her next to him when he turned over. But where was she? He started to get out of bed when she came into the room bringing him coffee.

"Morning, sleepy head. It's only six o'clock but I think you'd best be on your way. You don't want to ruin your reputation."

"What reputation?" he asked reaching for her. "I may spend the day right here. Did anyone ever tell you how beautiful you are first thing in the morning?"

"That's the first time I heard that today," she said as she reached down and gave him a kiss on the top of his head. "But you need to go home, change your clothes, and get to work."

"I didn't know you could be so bossy," he said with a smile.

"I got a lot to do before I can open today. So I got to get out of here too."

"Can I see you tonight?" he asked as he put his arms around her.

"I'll check my calendar," she said as she kissed him.

"Your neighbors will see me leave."

"I learned a long time ago not to worry about my neighbors. Anyhow, your car is pretty much hidden in the shrubbery in front of the house."

"I'll call you."

Andy practically floated back to Harry's house. By the time he got there, Andy was back in a working mood. He needed to talk with Mike. Maybe he, Andy, would buy all of Harry's stock in his greenhouse. He didn't want Harry to have any worries. But what would he do with them? He didn't think Mike had room for them. There was also the matter of Andy's penthouse plants. He might leave most of them there if he sold his place, but not his rose bushes. *Wait, what do I mean? Sell his penthouse? Did my night with Sarah completely...?* He hurried in the house to change clothes and get to work.

When he arrived at Mike Nelson's Landscaping he saw Mike's car already in the driveway. He entered the building but stopped in the office.

"You're here bright and early," Andy said to Mike.

"You, too, Andy. I'm still basking in the glow of Marv's knowledge. Gabe stayed all night nursing our rose bushes every two hours. I'm going to stay tonight."

"Then the next night will be mine," Andy said. "Marv's a wonder. You could almost see the wheels turning in his brain while he pondered what was wrong."

"I've been thinking of something. Have you ever seen his greenhouse? It's a shame he can't find a buyer for it all. Do you think we'd have room for it all or is it too big?" Mike asked.

"I'm not sure. I haven't seen it for a long time. I know he has also sold some of his holdings. I also have a problem. I have three beautiful rose bushes on my terrace along with a lot of other plants. Marv has been taking care of them. If I hold onto my apartment I need to find someone to take care of them." He sat quietly for a minute wondering what to do.

Finally he spoke, "My rose bushes were so beautiful. Marv took such good care of them even when he didn't know where I was. My name should never have been mentioned in connection with them. All I did was pay the bills. The rose bushes belong to Marv. In my thinking about what to do with my penthouse I always thought I'd return the roses to Marv. But now he'll have no place for them."

The men sat there quietly thinking as the workers arrived to begin their day. Finally, Andy spoke. "I must buy all of Marv's stock. I owe him this for running out on him. Even though I did run he stayed true to my plants. I owe him this." He thought quietly for a minute or so then asked Mike, "Do you know of any place they might have room for his stock? Maybe a friendly competitor?"

Mike spoke quietly. "I think we need to find a place to bring them here. Would that be possible?"

"It's possible, but where would you put them?"

"I'll turn that responsibility over to Gabe," he said with a smile. "He can work miracles."

"Could you find a place for my roses, too?"

"Like I told you, Gabe works miracles. I sent him home to sleep today since he flower-sat last night. We'll ask him tomorrow."

When Andy left the office he realized by bringing his roses to Nuna Lake, he was making a break with his penthouse. It is time to put it on the market, he thought. But would it also mean making a break with his limo, with his plane, (well, maybe not his plane), with his membership in all the New York associations, with his belongings in the penthouse.

He felt a bit overwhelmed as he went about his daily duties.

That night he went to see Harry.

"Well, well," Harry said. "I heard you brought someone from New York to Nuna Lake."

"I should have known you'd know all about it. Marvin Hartley is one of the outstanding rose men in the country. He also happens to be a friend of mine. The special roses at Mike's place got sick. And Marv did figure out what was wrong."

"Are the roses going to be okay?" Harry asked.

"They should be." Andy sat quietly saying nothing.

"You look troubled, Andy. Is it anything you can talk about? Please don't tell me you and Sarah had words," Harry said.

"Sarah is the brightest thing in my life right now. For the first time in my life, I think I'm falling in love with her. But I've made such a mess with my life. She deserves someone solid and steady in her life. I ran away from New York trying to get a new life in Nuna Lake, yet when I had troubles (both with Howie and then with the roses), I rushed back to my ties in New York to be able to help them. Does this mean I need to stay in New York or does it mean I need to hold onto those ties?"

"What does your heart tell you to do?"

Andy sat quietly with his head in his hand. "The only thing I know is that I don't want to be responsible for hurting Sarah. She deserves only the best. But I know she will never leave Nuna Lake. And right now I don't think I want to leave Nuna Lake. But I keep getting pulled back there."

"Maybe if you go back you'll find the answers," Harry said quietly.

"Maybe you're right," he said.

Andy had a restless night. He awoke tired and troubled. He didn't feel like going to work. He felt like he wanted to hide under the covers. He missed the smell of coffee that Harry usually had ready in the morning. He missed hearing the morning news on TV that Harry always listened to. What was he going to do? He thought about Sarah. He never expected to have a woman in his life. Sarah is so strong. Sarah is so independent. Sarah is so beautiful. Sarah is so loving. Sarah is… Andy had never felt so conflicted in his life. He had expected to have answers after his talk with Harry the night before but Harry didn't have the answers. No, he realized, this is one problem I need to settle by myself. I need to go to New York, talk with my broker and business manager, get every possible bit of information I can and then decide what to do with the rest of my life. He'd talk with Mike when he got to work. He might as well get this over with. Maybe it wouldn't hurt to let Sarah know. He reached for his phone.

"Good morning, Andy. Did you have a good night's sleep last night?" Sarah asked.

"Actually, no." he said. "I would have slept better if you were by my side."

"Talk like that makes me smile," she answered.

"Sarah, I think I need to go to New York. It has been six months since I left the city. I know I need to make some decisions about my life. But I know I want you with me. Can you get away and go with me to New York? I know you are so levelheaded that you will help me make the right decisions."

"Andy, I can't get away right now. We're still moving things at the store, I need to get my Christmas merchandise on the floor, and I'm opening up a new section.... I really need to be here." She was quiet for a minute. "I might try to influence you. I don't want to do that." She was quiet.

"Sarah, I think I'm in love with you."

"Andy, I think I'm in love with you." She paused for a moment. "Maybe with you gone for a few days we'll both have time to think about this."

"Can I still call you from New York?"

"Of course you can. Andy, I don't know anything about your first marriage and I'm not really interested in hearing about it. I also had a past full of memories. I swore I'd never get involved again. Maybe we both have things to think about."

"I'll call you."

"I'll be here."

Andy headed for work. When he went inside the building he saw Mike and Gabe in Mike's office standing over some blue prints of the plant.

"Andy, come in a minute," he heard Mike say.

"I've been doing some planning," Gabe said. "Take a look at this; if we move this over here and move this over there we can open up this area to accommodate most of Marv's holdings. At least most of them. Now, the roses are another matter. I think we should keep them all in the lab. If there's not enough room for them, maybe we can create another section next to it. Do you think it might work? Do you think our estimates of his holdings is close?"

"I really don't know. But I did reach a decision of sorts. I need to go to New York to settle some business matters. I need to bring an end to my so called experiment of coming to Nuna Lake. I need to be able to call this home," Andy said very quietly. "I need to put my penthouse on the market, get rid of the household items, and let go of New York. I know I'm still somewhat of a stranger here. If I need to move from here I will, but I don't think I could ever go back to living the life I had there."

There was a period of quiet in the room. Then Mike spoke. "Whether you like it or not, or whether it fits your plans for your future, you have become a Nuna Laker. I think Nuna Lake will be glad to have you here. Do you want to go to New York right away? How long will be you gone? Are you planning to leave right away."

"I might as well get it over with. I'll send for my plane today. I'll go see Marv right away and call you about the space. I'll get the plants on their way to you. Then I'll take care of my personal business. I won't have much to do there – someone will do it for me – but I'll have to go through my things."

He sat quietly for a minute and then said, "Do you think Harry will let me continue to live in his home for a while?"

"I'm sure he will, but it might be nice to ask him."

"I should be able to wrap up the business in a week."

"So.... Be back to work on time in a week."

"Mike, Gabe, you've both been so good to me..."

"Don't go getting mushy on us," Gabe said. "See you next week."

Andy went to see Harry.

"I'm going to New York today. The plane should be here this afternoon," he told Harry.

"Since I may be gone for a week or so, do you have any instructions about the house?"

"The house will be fine. Go to New York, take care of business and come back to Nuna Lake. We need you here."

Andy thought he might choke up when he heard the words. When if ever had he been told he was needed?

"You overrate me, Harry. But the more I think about this, I know it is the right thing to do. One thing is bothering me. Do you want me to leave your home?"

"Absolutely not," Harry said. "It is as much your home as mine. Stay as long as you want." Harry paused. "It makes me sad to think about having to sell the house, but I know I'll never be going back there. This is my home now. I do miss the house, miss seeing Millie cooking in the kitchen, and miss her in my bed at night….." His voice got softer as he remembered. But quickly he regained his composure. "Someday, before too long maybe, you'll decide to leave the house. But until you do decide to do that, think of that house as your home. I'm in no rush to see it gone."

"Harry, you're a special man. I'll call you and let you know how it's going. I plan to say goodbye to the penthouse when I leave, but I think I'll keep my broker and business manager. They take care of so many things for me."

"Will you be able to say goodbye to your friends this trip?"

"I have only two friends there – Marv, whom I'll be doing business with, and a sweet lady who cooked breakfast for me every morning."

Andy's next stop was at Sarah's shop. He found her knee deep in packing boxes.

"I'll be going to New York this afternoon," he told her.

"The sooner you leave the quicker you'll be back," she said as she rose to greet him.

"You're sure you can't leave and come with me?" he asked.

"It's best if I don't. You might miss your plane," she said with a grin.

"Maybe I might make the plane wait for me," he answered. "I'll call you when I get there. If you change your mind and want to join me, I'll send the plane back to get you."

She came to him for one last caress before he left. As he held her in his arms, he knew for sure he was making the right decision to leave New York. Nuna Lake would be his new home.

He made his way to the airport where Hank was waiting for him. He boarded his plane and sat in the co-pilot's seat. "I got the copy of your business plans. I read them and then sent them to my business manager to take a look at. He said it was a very well thought-out plan, covering almost everything. He especially liked it because you made plans for a catastrophic claim."

"Well, we tried to think of everything."

"Do you feel your reserves are a bit on the light side?"

"Yes, we would have been more comfortable if we allowed a larger amount, but feel we might be able to increase it in a year," Hank told him.

"My broker thinks it might be a good investment in six months. Do you feel comfortable making the move now?"

"We stand to lose a couple of contracts if we don't move quickly. Both of us own our homes so we can always mortgage them if we need more cash."

"Would it help you to have an emergency fund set aside? I think Nuna Lake needs to have airport services more easily available. I am willing to invest in your future because I think it will be good for Nuna Lake. It was so nice to have service available when I needed to go to Arizona for Harry. Or when we had another emergency with a child. I believe Nuna Lake needs air service more readily available." He paused, and then added. "Maybe I could build a hangar big enough for my plane to be stored."

"I'll share your thoughts with Joe. All joking aside, you really feel like this is a doable project for Joe and me?"

"I think it will be great for Nuna Lake.

Chapter 18

Andy took a cab from the airport to his penthouse. Somehow the idea of having a limousine and chauffeur to drive him seemed very phony and pompous. He decided to sell his limo. He knew that someone at the garage would do it for him. He must remember to make the call. The doorman at his building greeted him.

"Mr. Mellon, welcome home. It's been so long since we've seen you. If you need anything, please call the office."

Andy hurried to the private elevator which would take him to his penthouse. As he unlocked the door and entered he felt, well, he felt sort of out-of-place. It was not inviting at all. It reminded him of a hotel room, not a thing out of place, nothing personal lying around. Just 'politically correct for a man of means.' He reached for his phone. He had promised to call Sarah when he got there. He could hardly wait to hear her voice. Then he started to laugh. It had only been a few hours since she sent him on his way. *I must be in love,* he thought. He felt good. As he pressed in her number he looked around at the beauty of his penthouse. It was stiff and somewhat formal, but tastefully furnished. He should have no trouble selling it.

He looked into his kitchen. Somehow, the memory of Mima singing as she prepared his breakfast came to him. *She was the best thing about this place.*

"Sarah's Card and Gift Shop," he heard Sara's voice answering the phone.

"I love you, I miss you, and I'm in New York."

"Glad you had a safe trip. I'm with a customer right now. Can I call you right back about that order?"

"Yep, don't forget."

"I won't."

It was nearly six o'clock. Still early enough to call Marv and tell him he was in town.

"Marv, it's Andy."

"You're really here."

"Yes, I'm really here. We are serious about buying your stock. Could I come out tomorrow to see it and see how much space we need to arrange for it?"

"Of course you can. I'm an early bird so any time in the morning is good for me."

"Does your wife need someone with her while we look at your plants?"

"She'll be fine. She has missed seeing you. I told her you looked happy and healthy but she wouldn't take my word for it. She'll be glad to see you."

He hung up his phone and then dialed Mima's number.

"Hello."

"Hello, Mima, this is Andy Mellon."

"Andrew, Andrew, I mean Mr. Mellon, is it really you? Where are you? How are you? Do you need me to come over tonight?"

"Absolutely not. But call me Andy. All my friends do."

"I was so glad when Lauren saw you in Chicago. I had been very worried about you."

"I certainly should have called and let you know where I was. I guess she told you about me. Mima, I was hiding out. I was trying to run away from being Andrew Mellon, loner. Now I am Andy Mellon, a man with a 40-hour a week job. I get dirty going it. I have tons of friends. Mima, you'll be glad to know I've even fallen in love. She is so wonderful."

"I am so happy for you. Did she come to New York with you? I'd like to meet her."

"No, she couldn't get away so quickly. She has a card and gift shop in a little town called Nuna Lake."

"Are you planning to go back there?"

"Yes. I'm in town now to put my penthouse on the market."

"Then I must come there tomorrow to help you."

"That isn't necessary."

"I'll be there very early, say six-thirty, to help you."

"You'd do that for me?"

"Of course."

"How about waiting a day? I have an early morning appointment with Marv. I'm going to buy all the stock he has left in his greenhouse and ship it to Nuna Lake. It may take a while. But I definitely want to see you. Could you come at your regular time the next day?"

"Of course. Of course. Will you be staying there long? Should I buy you some groceries to have on hand?"

"No, I won't be staying too long. Just long enough to take care of business."

"Well, then, I'll see you the day after tomorrow. Andy, I'm so glad to hear from you. Have you talked with your friend, David Hass, lately?"

"Not for a while. Why do you ask?"

"That good doctor met my daughter when she went to observe an operation he performed."

"Yes, I remember that."

"Well, anyhow he was impressed with something she said and remembered her. He asked her if she would like to train in his specialty, and so she's in Chicago now working for him. He thinks very highly of you. And now he's being good to my daughter. She's very happy. You made it all happen for her and we both thank you for doing it."

"Your daughter must be very bright or David would not have asked her. He's a particular, fussy man, but a brilliant one. He must have seen something special in Lauren to have taken her on board."

"Well, she's very happy and I think she is doing well. I was so happy when she saw you at the hospital. I had been very worried about you."

"I should have called you, Mima. But I was feeling very depressed when I left. I saw a picture of Nuna Lake in a magazine and decided to go there and get a new life. I have never been happier."

"Then I'm happy for you. I'll see you day after tomorrow."

He ended the call and headed for his terrace to look at his roses. How beautiful the plants were. How healthy they were. He knew he owed Marv for their good condition. He lingered over then, touching each branch. There were still blooms on the roses in spite of the lateness of the season.

The plants looked very healthy. Marv had really looked after them well. There wasn't a sign of a disease or bug. They were truly beautiful. But what could he do with them. He knew they didn't really belong to him – they belonged to Marv. He would take them back to Nuna Lake. But is it really fair for him to take them when they really belonged to Marv? Maybe Sarah would know what to do. She was so smart.

"Hi" Sarah said when she answered her phone. "Did you see your beautiful rose bushes?"

"I did and they're perfect. Sarah, what am I going to do? They don't belong to me, they belong to Marv. And he's moving to a retirement community with no place for a garden. I gave them a home for a while but they are really his."

"Maybe the answer will come to you tomorrow," she said.

"I hope so," he replied. "Anything exciting happening in town?"

"Actually, yes. Remember I told you about the one-of-a-kind merchandise I carry?"

"Yea, the ones you don't make any money on."

"Yea, that group is what I'm talking about. Well, anyhow, I got a call from them today asking me about carrying a new product. It comes from one of the poorest section in Kenya. The area is very old world. There is no well in town to get their water. Little girls don't go to school because they have to carry water for the village. They carry those big jars on their head for almost ten miles from a well that was drilled in a neighboring village. It's a very, very, poor area. With no water in the village you can imagine the health and hygiene problems. Anyhow, on a trip there the group saw the villagers making a crèche, you know, the nativity scene we see at

179

Christmas time. They are very primitive and small. They're made from grasses, twigs, bark, leaves – you know – very primitive. Anyhow, the man told the villagers that he would try to sell the crèches and give them the money so they could drill a well in the village. A well costs at least $3000 and sometimes more. When the man came back to the village he found the villagers had made more than 1,000 of the crèches. Because I have been successful selling things from the area, he asked if I would try to sell one hundred of them. He had already shipped one to me overnight as a sample. I got it this afternoon. Andy, it is so beautiful. The characters are only a couple of inches high. The little manger is only about an inch high. They are packaged together in a box about 9x6x2 inches made from banana leaves. They are the sweetest things. The group paid $3 each for them and hope to sell them for $30 or so. If I sell them all, I will send them $3000. That's the price of a well. I'm so excited about them. I realize that I make nothing from selling them. But think what a well would do for the people of the village. They offered to send the crèches to me on consignment because I've sold so many of their items, but I decided I can afford the $300 so I offered to buy them. I'm really excited about it. I really think I can sell them. They faxed me the information so I decided that I will sell them on my internet site as well as in the store. Isn't that something? Can't you see the headlines in the paper? LITTLE NUNA LAKE DIGS A WELL IN AFRICA. She stopped talking and took a deep breath. "I'm sorry I've run on so. I'm just so excited to be a part of this."

"Little Sarah of "Little Nuna Lake" is doing this. Sarah, you are a wonderful, thoughtful, kind person. Some people would see this as an opportunity to get famous. You are loving, kind...."

"Don't stop talking," she said. "My head is beginning to grow bigger."

"As if it could," he said. "I really miss being with you for this big announcement."

"You'll be back soon. I'll be waiting for you."

"Love you, Sarah."

"Love you, Andy."

They said goodnight.

The next morning, Andy rose early and made his way to Marv's home. At one time Marv's home had been a farm. Eventually the lots were sold for subdivisions; only Marv's property remained as a small farm. He had erected a greenhouse on one side and it was in this building that Andy found the remains of Marv's stock of plants.

"I sold some more of the stock since I returned from Nuna Lake." Marv told him.

"Mike wants to buy your remaining stock. He has great respect for your work. But I want to buy them for me. I need to find out how much space we need to house them"

"It would give me great pleasure to give them to you or Mike. I really thought I'd be throwing them away."

"Marv, I owe you so much. Until I got away from New York I didn't realize what a recluse I had become. You and Mima were the only contacts I had with the outside world. And when I abandoned my penthouse, you stayed true to the beautiful garden and roses I had on my terrace. When I sell my penthouse, I'll take the roses, but the other plants will stay in their place.

If I buy your plants it will be like having a little bit of you with me. And I want that. I need that. I will keep them at Mike's for a while, but who knows. I may buy a house soon and if I do I will put these plants in my yard. It will be like having your blessing with me."

"You'll have your roses. I know you'll keep them."

"I'm greedy. I want more."

"You flatter me."

"You deserve it."

"I'll talk it over with Mother" Marv said. "Let's go in the house and have coffee while I think it over."

"Is she able to have company?"

"She loves company. She considers you one of her boys."

"Then let's go see her. Is it too early in the morning?"

"She told me to be sure to bring you in for coffee. We have a nice nurse here to attend to her medical needs. They both have been getting ready for you."

"Then let's go have coffee."

"It's so good to see you." Andy went to Marv's wife and gave her a hug as she lay in her bed.

"Andrew, it's so nice to see you. Marv told me you look just wonderful and now I can see it for myself. Marv really missed talking with you."

"I was your proverbial little boy who ran away from home. I should have called Marv, but somehow I couldn't talk to anyone. But running away led me to find a new way of life. I'm very happy there."

"Marv said you have some very nice friends. Did you know that a nice lady named Rose sent me soup, little cakes, and a bouquet of flowers?" she asked.

"I heard about that. I think that everyone in Nuna Lake has that kind of mentality. I've never seen a place like it in my life. That's why I came back to New York; not only to see about Marv's plants, but to get my personal things and put my penthouse on the market so I can officially move to Nuna Lake."

"Marv told me about your plans. I wish you every happiness as you put down roots in Nuna Lake. And I hope you've met a nice young woman to make a home with."

"I think I have. I think maybe I have."

"When do you think you will ship out the plants? "Marv asked.

"They will be packaged up today. Tomorrow we will package up the bushes in my penthouse. By the next day they will be in their new home in Nuna Lake. Or is this too soon for you?" Andy asked.

"No, it's not too soon. It will be one less thing I have to think about. Oh, I just remembered something." He left the room and came back with an envelope which he handed to Andy. "This just came yesterday from the Rose Society. You should fill out the papers and send them in."

Andy took a minute to look at the papers. He thought about the information requested on the forms. Then he quietly said to Marv, "Let's fill out these forms right now. He reached for his pen. He could see the letter was a registration form concerning the experimental roses: the roses Marv worked so hard to produce. Andy sat down at the dining room table and began to complete the form. The form asked for the name of the owner, grower, and developer of the plant. He filled in Marv's name in each category. There was one more line: the name given to the rose that was developed. He said to Marv, "What name do you want to call this rose?"

"It's your rose, you name it."

"It's a rose you took care of, fussed over, and loved. You should give it a name."

"No, you name it. It will grow in your yard. You must give it a name."

Andy thought for a minute. "Okay then, we will name the rose Maureen."

"Maureen? Maureen? But that's my wife's name."

"Exactly. Why shouldn't this rose have the name of someone you love?"

"Andrew, no, no," Maureen exclaimed.

"No, no," Marv almost shouted.

"I will take these roses back to Nuna Lake with me. They are really special because they should begin to bloom in late February or the first of March and bloom through to November or December. I will write up directions for their care. Then I will send a rose bush to each of your three children to plant in their yards. That way they will always remember their mother and father and the love they shared."

"No, no," Marv began to shout and then he looked at his wife. Tears were flowing from her eyes.

"Andrew, that is the most thoughtful thing you could ever do for us. The children will remember their father as he tended the plants. And if it has my name it will help them to remember me. Thank you, Andrew, thank you. Come here so I can give you a hug. I feel so honored," his wife said.

"Andrew, I'll never forget this kind gesture. However can I thank you?"

"By knowing that the beauty you brought us will live on for years after we are all gone."

Back in his penthouse that night, Andy began to look around to see what he would leave and what he would take back with him. He was a bit surprised that he wanted to take so little. About all of his clothes could go to the Salvation Army. So could the kitchen items. He looked in his desk. There wasn't too much there since his business manager took care of his spending. He found an empty box in the closet and put a few mementos inside the box. He looked around the place. The household linens, etc. could go with the house or to the Salvation Army. He wanted his break with New York to be complete. He went into his library. He had so many books which had given him pleasure. He decided he would take most of them with him to Nuna Lake. They had become like old friends to him. The remainder of the books could be given away.

In the back of the top shelf of the bookcase he found three shoe-box sized boxes. He looked inside one of them. The first thing he saw was a picture of his grandfather and grandmother. It had been years since he had seen the picture. They were seated on the swing on the front porch. They looked so proud and happy. He held the pictures close to his chest for a few minutes. Then he found pictures of his mother and father. They looked so young. There was a wedding picture of them. He found his baptism long white dress. He found all his report cards, his 4-H awards, his swimming award and other mementos of his youth. He found souvenirs that he remembered were from his father and mother. Memories began to flood his mind of stories that his grandparents had told him. *Why had I not looked in this box before?* he wondered. After sitting there a while, he put everything carefully away. He put the boxes close to his bed that night. They would go to Nuna Lake.

At 6:30 the next morning as he got up, he heard the keys in the door and knew Mima had arrived. He grabbed his robe and ran to greet her. He gave her a big hug as she came in the door.

"My, oh my," she said as he greeted her. "Such a welcome. I am so glad to see you, Mr. Mellon."

"You must call me Andy. All my friends do."

"You look just wonderful, so strong, so happy. Oh, I've missed you."

"Mima, I've told everyone that I only missed two people – you and Marv."

"Mr. Mel.., I mean Andy, you flatter me. But I am glad to see you. Now let me get busy and fix you breakfast. I brought eggs, sausage, bacon, and bread and butter with me. One day when I came over a few months ago, I threw out everything you had in the refrigerator."

"Mima, you and Marv were the only people I missed when I left New York. I should have stayed in touch." He stopped talking. "It took time for me to adjust to the world and somehow I felt if I came back here I would be back to my old ways, isolated from everyone. When I bought your daughter's old car it awakened me to a desire to change my life. And I did change my life. Nuna Lake was the right place for me to do it. You know, Mima, I think I was afraid of life – afraid of getting hurt – I don't know – just afraid. Yet I found the courage and I found a wonderful world out there full of wonderful people. I really missed you and Marv, but I really had no life to leave behind."

"You are going to make me cry," she said. "So instead, sit right down here while I fill your plate. You look like you're eating well these days. How long will you be in town?"

"Just a couple of more days. I've had many decisions to make. I have a good stock broker and business manager. But I can live anywhere and keep them. I think I want to keep my plane. The two pilots I hired may purchase the air field near Nuna Lake. If they do, I'll take my plane there. There were a couple of occasions when the people of Nuna Lake needed to use a plane in an emergency. I'd like to provide that."

"Then you're planning to go back to Nuna Lake."

"Yes," he answered quietly. "I'll be going back in a day or so. But I will not need this penthouse any longer so I'm going to sell it."

"What about your roses?"

"I'm taking them back with me this trip. I'm not sure where they'll end up, but I work for a man in the nursery business."

"Does he know you're a man of means?"

"Yes, he knows. I didn't tell anyone who I was at first. I was Andy Mellon, a drifter. But the town welcomed me. Everyone was so good to me. I roomed in a house with an old man whose family didn't want him to live alone. He became like family to me. I made friends with the people I work with, and Mike Nelson, who owns the nursery where I work, and his wife are kind and welcoming. I made friends with almost everyone in town. It's a unique kind of place: one where no one asks about your business, yet everyone in town seems like one big family."

"And I hope that's where your nice single lady lives." Mima said.

"She does, indeed. Her name is Sarah. She is the kindest, smartest woman I ever met. And she has a heart of gold. She runs a card and gift shop. I know I love her, but she was hurt by a man in the past. She is very independent, strong and doesn't need anybody. But I'm hoping she'll want me."

"Of course she'll want you."

"Mima, did I ever tell you I love you," he said with a laugh.

"Treasure your Sarah. Love her. Spend the rest of your life with her." Mima sat quietly for a minute then spoke.

"What can I do to help you get this place ready to go on the market?"

"I think I'll leave everything as it is except for personal items. I really didn't have too many things around."

"I believe there are personal items on your bookcase shelves. I just dusted around them recently."

"I found the boxes last night. They are special things that I'll take with me."

"What about your garden?"

"I'm going to take the roses with me. We'll find a home for them at the place where I work. The larger plants will stay for the next owner."

"Your breakfast is ready now. Sit right down while I serve you."

"I want you to sit and talk with me while I eat. Is there anything in this apartment that you would like to have?"

"Not a thing. I have good memories of you. That is enough. I certainly will miss you when you're gone."

"Mima, I have made arrangements for you to have a pension from me for the rest of your life. They will mail you a check each month. Maybe with your daughter in Chicago now you will come to the mid-west to see Lauren and you can visit Nuna Lake. You would really like it there."

"You don't need to provide for me, Mr...Andy. I'm going to be fine."

"I know I don't need to, but I want to. Let me do this for you. You were the one person who kept me sane through all my trials with Gretchen. I didn't realize at the time how much I depended on you. You are a very special lady."

They were interrupted by the intercom from the lobby of his building.

"There's a man here who says he is supposed to package your rose bushes for shipping. Shall I let him come up?" the doorman asked.

"Yes, let him in."

Andy now realized that this was actually happening. He would be leaving New York behind.

That afternoon he went to see his business manager to tell him he was moving but would still like his services. He asked the man about the help given to the New York City children when it rained. "I don't remember ever hearing about that before."

"It was listed on the reports I sent you quarterly under donations. I want to be sure you reach the maximum allowed under charity giving to be claimed on your income tax."

"I guess I never read them properly," Andy said. "Please continue that practice," he told the man.

"Any other special instructions for me?" the business manager asked.

"I appreciate all the behind the scene work you did when I needed money for the Children's Hospital a few months ago"

"It was a good thing you called me to let me know. I probably would have called the police. It had been some time since I had heard from you. If I had started to get bills from Chicago without knowing you were there I probably would have thought you were kidnapped. I did wonder what you were up to."

"A car crashed into a town park. Three people were killed and one little boy was terrifically injured. I called a doctor, an old friend, who performed surgery on him. No one in town knew at that time who I was. My friend, the doctor, told the people a benefactor would pick up the bill. But we were told that Nuna Lake takes care of its own. I couldn't interfere without revealing who I was. I wasn't ready to do that. Collection jars were placed all over town with a note that money collected would go to pay for the boy's care. I did put in a lot of hundred dollar bills in the jars. But it's only because you paid the balance so discretely after I called you that I could relax. The hospital was also very discrete. Nuna Lake got all the credit for paying the bill. But that reminds me. I would like to establish two scholarships to be awarded to the high school graduating class in the spring in memory of the two young boys who were killed that day. Can you make those arrangements?"

"Sure. I'll put together some ideas for them and send them to you. Do you need them before spring?"

"That'll be fine. Another thing, what did you really think of Joe and Hank's plan to buy the airfield?"

"I looked into quite a few things before I decided, but I think it could turn out to be a good investment. With all the on-line shopping these days, home deliveries are way up. It does appear that the area needs a drop zone for shipments. If Joe and Hank are there, ready to receive the packages, I believe the prospects for investments are good. But tell me, Andrew, do you plan to stay in Nuna Lake?"

"Right now, I believe I do. But please call me Andy. I'll be going back to Nuna Lake tomorrow. Let me give you my cell number so you can call me if anything comes up."

After leaving the office, he called his broker to inform him of the move.

"Do you want to transfer the management of your account to Nuna Lake?" the man asked.

"No, you have made me a rich man. I want you to continue to do so."

He called the airport and made arrangements to fly back to Nuna Lake the next afternoon.

I'm really doing it. This is the real beginning of a new life in Nuna Lake.

Chapter 19

Well, this is it, Andy thought as he fastened his seat belt. *I'm officially leaving New York. Does this automatically make me a Nuna Laker? It's funny; I don't have any feelings about leaving New York. I do think it is the right thing for me to do. I said my goodbyes to Mima and Marv. They are probably the only ones who even care to know where I am. They are such nice caring people. I guess there are nice people in New York. I just never got to know them. I have many acquaintances in New York, but very few I could call a friend. But now it's on to my new life in Nuna Lake.*

He was sitting behind the pilot of the small cargo plane he had rented so that all the plants he was taking to Nuna Lake could be taken with him. He thought about all his new friends – too many to count. He still had moments when he felt like an outsider but they were few and far between all the rest of his good thoughts. Things had gone well with the closing of his penthouse. Since the landlord had a waiting list of people who wanted to move there, he knew it would sell quickly.

He thought about Sarah. He had really missed her even though it had only been a couple of days. He missed her smile.

He missed her logical good sense about life. He missed… well, it would only be a matter of a couple of hours before he would see her. He loved her enthusiasm for life and for people. He knew he wanted to marry her, but he knew she was an independent woman. Would she want to keep things as they were? He knew he loved her. If that's the best she can give me, can I accept that? He wanted to take care of her, but would she let him? She was so independent. She was so kind and giving. Maybe she'd say no to marriage. Could he ever just be her friend? Yes, he thought. If that's the best she can give me, I'll take it.

When the plane arrived back in Nuna Lake he saw a big truck waiting for them. He oversaw the transfer of all the plants to the truck and then went for his car. *Maybe it is time I buy a new car,* he thought. But the old Ford Escort still worked well. For a moment he thought about his arrival in Nuna Lake all those months ago. He had been so depressed and discouraged with his life. Now he felt like he was coming home. He got in his car and reached for his phone. She picked up on the first ring.

"Is this my beautiful Sarah?" he asked.

"Words like that will get you a really nice, warm welcome," she said.

"I can hardly wait to see you, but I need to go now to help unpack the cargo I brought back."

"I'm anxious to hear all about your trip. Want to come for dinner tonight? I bought some steaks."

"I'd love that. What time? Do you need to close the store tonight or is Julia there?"

"Wait a minute." He heard her talking to Julia.

"Julia said she'll stay late tonight so come over when you leave the nursery."

"See you soon."

He followed the truck as it made its way through town. Mike had a crew meet them to unload the plants. They carefully put them in place.

"I'm really anxious to see the roses. Oh, my," Mike said. "I can't believe this. It's late November. These roses are still blooming. I can't believe it," he repeated.

"I've never seen roses like these," Gabe added. "They look like they have ruffles on them. Did you ever see anything like that?"

The three men stood looking at the bushes. They were full of roses. It was past the middle of November, the air was cool, yet these roses bloomed on.

"I can't believe this," Gabe added. "And I don't think I've ever seen a rose like this. How did you develop ruffles or even this color? It's so unique."

The rose had a deep purple throat that fanned out, fading gently from the deep color to a pale lilac petal with a fringe look on the outer edge. It was very unique and very beautiful.

"How did you do that?" Mike asked.

"It was all Marv's plan to do this. It involved some cross-breeding with another flower. I'm not sure how he did it, but these rose bushes were his special baby. I'm sure he hated to see them go, but he insisted I take them all. I know he could have sold them for a lot of money. I registered them with the Rose Society before I left New York and listed Marv as the owner, grower and developer. That will protect his name. We named the rose "The Maureen". It's the name of his wife."

"I bet that name was your idea," Mike said to Andy.

"It is a tribute to Marv and his wife," Andy answered quietly.

Mike kept looking at the other plants. "These are all beautiful plants. They are really healthy looking. I'm ready to house them as long as you like, but I know you could get top dollar for them if you want to sell them."

"Mike, these are your plants. They are my gift to you for taking a chance on hiring me. I had no experience and yet you took a chance. This group of rose bushes is another story. They are the special ones Marv was developing – Marv had three at his greenhouse and I had three at my place. They were developed to start blooming by the end of February. They will bloom in the fall season until late October or early November. I plan to package and send a rose bush to each of Marv's three children. I also have plans for the other three: one is for you to plant in Rose's garden, one is for Gabe who loves all plants, and the other is for me. Who knows, one of these days I may move from Harry's but if not I'll plant it in his yard."

"You can't give them to us. I'll pay for the plants. I'll even pay for the rose bushes. It is so nice for you to share them. And it's nice you thought of Marv's kids. I'll be thrilled to have one in our yard," Mike said.

"It's my way to say thank you. By giving me a job, you gave me a life. Going back to New York made me realize how much of a recluse I had become. I had no life at all. But now I look forward to each day. You gave me a chance to have a normal life."

"Nuna Lake feels like you always lived here," Mike said. "You're one of us now. But I have a hunch you might be anxious to go see a certain lady, so go now. I'll put these plants to bed for the night and see you in the morning."

"You are so right, Mike. Thanks. I'll see you tomorrow."

He got in his car and headed for Sarah's. He took a chance that she might have gone home early so went straight there.

She heard him pull in her driveway and came to meet him. They embraced. "It feels like five or six weeks you have been gone," she said.

"More like six months, I think. Sarah, I really missed you. I've always been so independent. I didn't think I needed anyone. But I need you, Sarah. I really need you. But more than that, I love you, Sarah."

She spoke quietly. "I've never felt real love before. It scares me but I love you too. I want to be with you, to share life with, to....."

He kissed her passionately. "I never thought I'd hear those words from anyone," he said.

"Nor did I," she said.

Chapter 20

Andy felt so completely happy he didn't think he could stand it. He knew there were things that needed done, but he couldn't keep his mind on them. The evening before had not gone exactly as he thought it would, but it ended perfectly. Sarah did have to return to the shop. He went with her. Sarah was keeping her shop open until 9 o'clock. She called them Christmas hours. That night she was so busy at work with customers. He had never seen the shop this crowded. People were buying their Christmas cards and looking at gift items. He knew Thanksgiving would be here in a few days. He thought that started the shopping season. But as he watched the people, he saw how excited they would get over a gift item or maybe finding the perfect card for 'Uncle Whoever.' He saw a small crowd around one table so he slowly made his way there. He saw Sarah at her best, doing what she loved. She was showing a group of customers the Christmas Crèches she was selling to earn money for a well in Africa. He heard her tell how every dime they paid for the set was going back to Africa to drill a well for water. She held up the tiny figures, one by one, explained where they came from, and reminded the people that she would not make any money by selling them. All the money would go directly to the people there.

"I'll take three sets," Andy heard one woman say. "I want each of my married children to have one."

"I'll pay $50 for one set," said one man. 'Send the extra money to Africa.'

And so it went. By the time the store closed fifteen sets had been sold; nearly $700 had been collected. Sarah was ecstatic.

"I want five," Andy told Becky, the high school girl who was helping. "Here's $200. Keep the change for the fund."

Becky looked up to see Sarah coming her way. She was aware of his feelings for Sarah and hesitated to take his money.

"He wants to buy five."

"Oh really," Sarah said with a smile. "And may I ask if you plan to give them to your girl friends."

"Well," Andy said slowly, "I guess I do. So here is one for under your Christmas tree. Two of them I'll ship to New York for Mima and Marv, one is going to Judy, Hobie and Katie, and one is for Harry."

Sarah reached out to give him a hug and a quick kiss. "I'll always treasure it."

For a moment Andy was taken back. It wasn't the acceptance of the gift; it was that she very publicly showed her affection for Andy.

He looked at Becky and said, "Do you think she'd do that again if I buy her another one?"

Becky stated to laugh. "Seems to me it would be worth trying." She turned to Sarah. "Why don't you two go home? I'll stay and help Julia close the store."

"I'd like to do that," Sarah said. "Good night everybody. Just close the store. I'll clean up in the morning."

"Good night, Sarah. Good night, Andy," they all told them.

"Good night, you good people. I love you all."

They didn't make it to the car before they stopped and kissed passionately.

"I really love you, Andy."

"I really love you, Sarah."

"Let's go home."

The next morning Sarah was surprised to get a call from Sam Watson, who published a weekly newspaper for the citizens of Nuna Lake. The daily paper came from Sprucedale.

"Good morning, Sarah. The town is abuzz about some hand-made crèches you are selling. Something about wells in Africa."

"Yea, Sam. We had quite a night. Would you like to see them? Stop by the store. Maybe I can sell you a dozen," she said with a laugh.

"I want to talk to you about that. Can I stop by for a talk in about half an hour?"

"I'll be here," she answered.

When he came to the store he was surprised to see how small the crèche was. "Just imagine someone sitting there creating this set. I'm really touched. I have an idea to present to you. I'd like to do an article next week featuring the crèches. I've talked to a couple of people. We'll use a picture of them and suggest people buy them. If someone doesn't want one, we'll suggest they can contribute to the "Nuna Lake Drills a Well in Africa" fund. Nuna Lake always responds to a good cause, and this is one everyone can get in on. People will be in a giving mood. Would you be agreeable to our doing this?"

"I'd be thrilled," Sarah said.

"I think it is something that we can do as a community. That's what I'm looking for. We don't seem to be having any "Nuna Lake Emergency Fund Raising Events" right now. I think this is one that would make everyone feel good. And you know, T'is the Season."

"Sam, I could kiss you for thinking of it."

"Well, I would enjoy that, but I have a feeling a certain man might not. Tell me, Sarah, are things serious between you and Andy?"

"Time will tell."

"I think he has been very good for Nuna Lake. I hope he stays around. Rumor has it that he might stay in town because of you. Is there a story here I should know about?"

"Andy is a very good, kind, and caring guy. I'm glad I know him."

"And I suppose you'll tell me that's the end of the story. Well, if there's any news, be sure to tell me first."

That night Andy helped Sarah close the store.

"I've got to tell you something. Rose stopped by the shop today. She bought five crèche sets: one for her mother, one for each of their kids, and one for her. She has invited us to share Thanksgiving with them. Their three kids are going to be there so it should be a fun time. Is it okay if I accept the invite? If you don't want to go, I'll cook a turkey."

"After the week you've had, you shouldn't have to cook. I'll be proud to go with you wherever you want to go."

"Good, because I already accepted for us."

"You think you know me pretty well, don't you?" he asked.

"Yes. I know exactly who you are and I love you."

Andy fussed over what to wear to Thanksgiving dinner. He decided to put on jeans and a sweater. He felt a great sense of relief when he picked up Sarah and she was also in jeans and a sweater. When they arrived at Mike and Rose's house they were greeted with hugs and kisses by Tim, Jeff and Karen, and Jenny, their adult children.

"I'm glad you're finally here," Rose said. "These kids of ours tell us they each have big news for us but made us wait till you got here. I've got dinner on the table so let's sit and eat before it gets cold."

As they finished desert, Tim, the son of Mike, stood up and taking a spoon in his hand hit the water glass.

"Since I'm the youngest, and the most handsome man here, I get to go first. I have big news for everyone. I have decided to leave school in Berkley, California. Now don't panic, Dad," he said while he looked at Mike, "it's all good. I am going to join an international group to work on a project about rain forests. Three other members of my group at school are going. We were selected based on our grades and interests. We might be gone for more than a year. But here is the good news. We are going to South America. The project is really, really interesting and I'm excited to be chosen so I said I would go. I don't have too many more courses left before I graduate, but if I wait until spring when I graduate, it will be too late to be with this study. It's so interesting." He sat back down in his chair.

"Tim, I don't know what to say," Mike sat there with a puzzled look on his face. "My first thought is that you're still my baby and I want you no farther away than California." He paused; everyone was quiet for a minute as they absorbed the news.

"Rosie, what do you say?" Tim asked.

"I can't bear the thought of you being so far away, Tim."

"I think it's great. You'll learn so much, not only about rain forests, but about conservation, about the people there, their customs, their family life. I think it's wonderful. I wish I could go too," said Jenny, Rose's daughter. "Mike, you've got to let him go. He might never get a chance like this again."

Jeff, Rose's son spoke up. "What about your girl friend? I thought you two were pretty serious."

"She's not too happy about it. I think she'd like to get married now. But if I don't accept this offer. I might never get this chance again. If she really loves me, she'll understand."

Then Mike spoke very quietly. "Tim, I remember when you were born. Your mother was so ill. She asked me to take care of you always, but to be strong enough to let you try new things, see and do new things. I guess I can't say you shouldn't go. So to honor your mother, I'll say I am very proud of you. And as I remember it, I was also afraid the day you learned to walk, or your first day of school, or your first night at Berkley so far away from home. I love you son." He got up from the table to give his son a hug, while the others gave their blessings to him.

"What's up with you, Jenny?" Tim said, anxious to get the attention away from him.

"Well, certainly nothing as earth-shattering as that, but I do have some good news. As you know, I'm on my way to becoming a doctor. I've now completed most of my book studies and I am being assigned to a hospital starting in January. I applied to several hospitals and was accepted at a couple, but I decided on Mercy General in Chicago. It's not the biggest or most prestigious, but it's a place that has the greatest need. They work mostly with the poor and needy. I know it won't look as good on a resume, but I feel like I'm needed there. It sort of reminded me of my days in Africa. I hope you're okay with my choice."

"I want you to always be happy," Rose said, going to give her daughter a hug. "I'm very proud of you. I had no idea you were thinking along these lines."

"We're all proud of you," said Mike.

"Does this mean you'll be able to take care of me in my old age?" Tim asked Jenny.

"Only if you promise to send me money when you're rich and famous."

Then Jeff spoke. "Well, my news sounds like nothing after what I've heard here, but Karen and I have news too, and no, it is not that we are pregnant. I'm changing jobs. I received an offer from another bank. I have decided to accept the offer. It is a big promotion for me. We will be moving from Chicago. I start my new job on January 2nd."

"Tell us, tell us, where is this new job," they seemed to ask in unison.

"Karen, you tell them," he told his wife with a smile.

"We are moving to.....Nuna Lake."

Everyone began to talk at once. When did all this happen, did he get a raise, when were they moving, etc? Jeff began to laugh

"Don Cunningham contacted me about three months ago. He said he had recommended me for the job. Remember when I met with him for advice about changing jobs, Mom? Well, I guess the Trust Officer at the bank is retiring, and Don recommended me. It's a big deal for me. Karen had to quit her job. This job will be challenging for me, moving and all. All together it seems like something big, but I know I'll have help from all of you."

"Karen, do you really want to quit your job? There are no jobs here for a department store buyer. You've been so successful; you must hate to quit," Rose asked.

"I was very glad to see Jeff get this offer. I know he's qualified and will be terrific at it. I'll be a little farther from my folks, but I want Jeff to be happy. Anyhow, I love working at Sarah's and hope she won't mind my being around there sometimes."

"I love having you around the shop," Sarah said. "Can you start work tomorrow? The store is a mess from a busy day yesterday."

"Mom told us about your "Wells for Africa" project. The crèches are so delicate and beautiful. I'll never forget my trip to Africa. I hope to go back someday. Those people are so satisfied with practically nothing, that you feel like you want to give them the world," Jenny said quietly, remembering her trip there.

Everyone then began to talk all at one time.

Andy had sat there listening to all this personal family talk. He had never heard anything like it. He realized something as he sat there. This family is Sarah's family. She had no brothers or sisters. I didn't either. She did have her mother for most of her life. All of Nuna Lake is Sarah's family, with Rose and Mike being the closest. She was very close to Rose, Mike and their family. Would they approve of him as suitable for her? He decided to quit being the little mousey man he had become and to speak up.

"Well, I guess it's my turn," Andy said. "I came to town as a stranger and you took me in without knowing anything about me. But I was a lonely man, used to being with many acquaintances, but few real friends. I made friends here, but the person who really changed my life from loneliness to bliss was meeting Sarah. I see only good in this woman. And though I haven't known her long, I know she is the most caring, compassionate woman I have ever met. When I came to Nuna Lake I only expected to stay for a few days. I have never seen a town so caring and compassionate; good people trying to provide good times for everyone. I want to make Nuna Lake my home."

Everyone was quiet for a minute and then Tim spoke. "Let's give three cheers for Sarah: Hip Hip Hooray, Hip Hip Hooray, Hip Hip Hooray."

Sarah said. "Thank you, thank you. Now let me help you get the pie, Rose. Come on everybody. Carry out your dirty plates to the kitchen sink."

Andy was quiet as they drove home. "Sarah, I hope I didn't embarrass you with what I said at the table, or maybe put you in an awkward position. I guess it just poured out of me. But I did mean it. I love you Sarah, but I don't want you to ever be uncomfortable because of me or something I might say. Sarah, I want you in my life forever. I love you. I want to marry you. I want to take care of you even though I know you take care of everyone else."

"With you in my life everything has been so good," she quietly told him. "But I made a mess of things when I was younger. I swore I'd never let anyone get close to me again. I would be a strong independent woman who needed no one."

"Do you still feel that way?" he asked as he pulled into a parking lot.

She sat in the car quietly staring straight ahead. Then she turned to him. Taking his hands in hers she looked him in the eyes and said "I love you, Andy." She was quiet for a minute and then said, "I want to be your wife. I want the world to know what a good, decent, kind man you are. I'm embarrassed that the town knows about my past life, yet I know the town is here for me. Are you sure you could stand to hear any snide remarks that might be made about my past? I don't want you ever to be embarrassed or ashamed of me."

"I could never be ashamed of you, Sarah. And if I'm not big enough to take anything that might be said, I'm not man enough to have someone as wonderful as you for a wife."

"Then my answer is yes."

The snow had begun to fall; it glistened on the trees lining the area, there was soft music on the car radio. "I don't think I have ever been this happy in my life. I feel like the luckiest man in the world," Andy said as he reached to embrace her. "Let's get married tomorrow."

"Let's enjoy each other tonight," she answered.

Chapter 21

Sarah woke in the morning to a bright sunshine coming in the window. It glistened on the light snow which lined the branches of the trees in her front yard. *I have never felt so much joy and happiness in my life,* she thought. *He loves me. He said he loves me.*

"I'm not asleep," Andy said as he pulled her closer to him.

"It feels so good to just lay here in your arms."

"Was it a dream last night or did you say you would marry me?"

"I hope it wasn't a dream. I want to marry you. I thought I'd never, ever get married. I can't believe it yet."

"Can we get married today?"

"Ha, Ha, Ha," she said in a terse kind of way.

"I mean it. I don't want to wait any longer. I am so happy you said yes. I want everyone to know you said it."

"I think I know who we should tell first."

"So do I. Shall we go tell him this morning? They start serving breakfast at seven at the home. He's probably the first one there. Harry is going to be so happy. He'll probably want to take credit for making me ask you."

"Or he may want to take credit for making me say yes."

"He's a schemer, that's for sure. Shall we get dressed and go see him? Or do you need to get to the shop. I know it will be a big day for you. It will for me too. I have to go shopping for an engagement ring. Any idea what kind of a ring you want?"

Sarah sat quietly for a minute or so. "Don't go shopping today. Let me think on it. But I do need to get to work. This weekend will probably be my biggest one of the year. Let's grab a coffee on our way to see Harry."

Harry was in the dining room eating his breakfast when Sarah and Andy come into the room. The room was more than half full of residents. They walked right to his table where he sat with his three buddies.

"The beaming light and aura around you can only mean one thing – she said "yes."

"Harry, you old coot, you are absolutely right," she said giving him a hug.

"Andy, you are a good man but I have to ask – you will take good care of her won't you?"

"Harry, I really love her. I want to be by her side forever."

"Then you've made this old man very happy. Sarah has always been like a daughter to me. I worried she would never want to be married."

"I never wanted to married," she said quietly. "But I know this: I know I want Andy by my side for all the days of my life."

She reached out and gave Harry a hug. "We've got to go now. I want to get breakfast before I go to the shop. But we wanted you to be the first to know."

"I repeat myself. You both have made this old man very happy. Andy if you have time today will you come back here later? I have some business to discuss with you."

"Of course, Harry. I'll see you in an hour or so."

"Want to stop at the diner?" Andy asked Sarah as they left Harry.

"I better just pick up breakfast and take it with me. I didn't clean up very well when we left the shop on Wednesday. I had planned to go back on Thursday, but my plans changed."

Julia had just arrived at the gift shop when Andy and Sarah got there.

"You two look positively beaming. Did you have a nice holiday?" she asked.

"It was a very usual day," Sarah said nonchalantly. "Andy asked me to marry him and I said yes."

"You what" Julia screamed. "Oh, Sarah, I'm so happy for you," She gave Sarah a hug.

"Tell me all about it."

"We better talk later. This store is a mess. Let's just shove the big things in place so we can open on time."

"You could be right. Joe and Martha were looking in the window when I got here. I suggested they get coffee and come back in fifteen minutes.

But if they thought they might be able to keep the engagement secret, in their bliss they had forgotten that there are no secrets in Nuna Lake. All day long Sarah had people wishing her much happiness. She laughingly said she thought the news brought her more business. Rose, Jennie and Karen stopped by. They had already heard the news and came to share her happiness.

Business really boomed. Andy brought lunch for them to eat in the back room, but insisted he would take everyone out to eat at eight o'clock when they closed the store. Everyone wanted to know the full details about the engagement. The full Christmas Shopping Season really began that day. It turned out to be best day ever for Sarah's shop.

Andy had also had a busy day. When he stopped at the jewelry shop to look at rings, of course, word about the engagement spread from shop to shop. He thought about his two best friends in Nuna Lake: Mike and Gabe. He called each one of them.

"Andy, I'm very happy for you," Gabe said when he heard the news. "Sarah is a wonderful person who deserves a good man. And I am happy it is you. I know you will take good care of her."

Andy waited until about 11 o'clock and then headed back to talk to Harry.

"I bet everyone in town will stop by Sarah's today," Harry said.

"I've never seen anything like it. People stopped by the shop even before she had officially opened the doors," Andy said.

"It's one the big mysteries of Nuna Lake; no one gossips but everyone knows everything." Harry said quietly

"What's on your mind? Is everything going okay here? Do you need anything?"

Harry sat quietly for a minute or so and then started to talk.

"I want to thank you for coming to live with me in the house I loved. I know I probably would have had to move away from there if you had not come to live with me."

"I assure you, the pleasure is all mine. You helped me to have a normal life. I am very happy to be marrying Sarah. But living with you for a while reminded me of all the good things in life instead of the lonely life I lived in the city. I owe you more than I can say."

"I need to talk about my house. Now I know that you have the money to buy it from me, and you might be thinking you should, but that would not be good. I know Sarah loves her house. She's had many offers from people to buy it. You two should live there. It's closer to her shop, has been updated to stay in good shape, and like I said, she loves her house. I need to put my house on the market. I'm getting very satisfied living in this home. Going forward I know I will probably need more and more help. I have decided it is time for me to sell my house. I need your help. After you and Sarah are settled in would you help me to make decisions about what needs to be done to the house to get it ready for the market? I don't need to make any money on the sale but I can't bear the thought of someone looking at it and picking apart the things that need done, or that they don't like. My children should not have to worry about it either. My children have moved so far away. I don't know who to turn to for help."

Andy could see that this was really worrying Harry. He sat quietly for a minute. "Harry, I love your house. I could buy it and be very happy living there. I have a feeling that Sarah would love it too. We've never talked about where we will live. It's all too soon for that."

"You aren't going to wait a long time to get married are you?" he asked.

"Not if I can help it. But Christmas season is a big selling season for her. I would be very disrespectful to her to push her on anything right now. I hope to be married to her before the first of the year. But this is a big season for her shop. And she's so involved with the Chamber of Commerce with Christmas plans; she's on a committee from her university that keeps her busy. And she's working with the schools on a mentoring program. I don't know how she does it all." He sat quietly for a few minutes.

The nurse's aid came into the room to take Harry to lunch. He was doing some walking on his own, but it was a long hallway to the dining room.

"Let me think on this for a couple of days."

"You will relieve my mind. I've thought of little else the last few days."

"I'll stay in touch."

Andy went home and took a good look at Harry's house. He tried to see the house without furniture for most of the furniture was aged and out of date. But the bones of the house were good. All the basement walls were dry and showed no signs of leakage anywhere. The roof had been replaced within the past three years. The furnace and air conditioner were only two years old. The windows showed some wear, and they were a bit on the small size, not like the modern big windows. The plumbing had all been replaced about eight years ago. Harry had taken good care of his house. But the furniture was old and comfortable. Hardwood floors had been covered with rugs and carpeting which needed replaced or removed. Harry should be able to get a good price on the house. Is it best to call a realtor, if so, which one? Andy thought long and hard about whether or not he should be the one to sell the house? Will Sarah want to stay in her own house? It's a smaller house to take care of, it was closer to her shop, and she had grown up in the house. He knew he could make no decisions before talking with Sarah.

At 7:30, he headed for Sarah's Card and Gift Shop. He had said he would take all the help out to eat after work. When he arrived at the shop it was still full of people. Anyone not busy with a customer was busy trying to tidy up the shop. Sarah came to greet him with a smile.

"Well, I guess everyone in town knows I'm going to get married. I can't believe how many people we had in here today. It's been one of my best day's ever. Oh, yes, we sold 27 crèches. Isn't that wonderful. The people were very generous when paying for them."

"I made reservations for us at Russell's. Can everyone leave right now?"

"This is so nice of you. They are all talking about going there tonight. But I'll either have to come back here tonight or come in early tomorrow to re-stock the shelves. We've had quite a day. What did you do today?" she asked as they walked to Russell's.

"Well, I looked at engagement rings for one thing. Nothing there was good enough for you."

"Well, I want a ring so big and heavy I have to have someone walking behind me to lift my arm. Surely you can provide me with something that size."

"You think you're funny, ha ha," he said in a droll fashion.

"You don't think that's funny? Where did my sense of humor go? Ah, me," she said with a sigh. "Really, Andy, I don't think I want an engagement ring. If I get a big diamond ring, people who shop here will think I'm being pompous and won't come back. If I get a small diamond people will think we're cheap. So let's skip the engagement ring. Just a nice gold band will be just super for me. Tell me, what did you do today besides look at rings?"

"Well, Harry has decided for us that I will move into your house and he will sell his house. I can't decide if it's a good or bad idea. It might bring him some relief to know it's been sold but it's where he had so many good memories of Millie."

"I'd say you got a problem to think about," Sarah said as they entered the restaurant. While she was there her cell phone rang. It was Rose.

"Can you talk for just a minute," she asked.

"Andy brought us all to Russell's for food."

"That's great. I just wanted to tell you that Jenny, Karen, and I will be at your shop at 6:30 tomorrow morning to straighten stock and refill shelves for the day. So ask Andy to be at the shop with keys to let us in."

"You can't do that."

"Of course we can. We might even bring the guys with us. We want to do this to help you. So don't say no."

"Rose, did I ever tell you I love you. We'll be there at 6:30."

"Who was that on the phone?" Andy asked.

"Just Rose. She and her troop are going to be at the shop at 6:30 in the morning to help re-stock shelves and tidy the place up."

"I guess that means I have to get up early, too."

"Aren't you glad you know me," she said as she cuddled in his arms.

"I'll let you know about ten o'clock tomorrow morning when I wake up," Andy said.

Chapter 22

The next morning when Julia and the staff arrived they found the floors swept. Counters were neat and the shelves were stocked.

"I can't believe this. Did you stay all night?" they asked.

"We had a lot of help here at 6:30 this morning. I can't believe how much we sold yesterday. If you're not busy with customers this morning, will you please see what we need to order. I thought I had enough for at least a week, but now I'm not so sure."

"I'll get right on it," Julia said. "Why don't you take a break and get something to eat. All of you," she said to Mike and Rose's family. "We can cover the store for at least twenty minutes."

The eight of them made their way down the street: Mike, Rose, Tim, Jennie, Jeff, Karen, Andy and Sarah.

"Coffee, coffee, coffee," Tim called out as they walked into the restaurant.

"You're all here early this morning," the waitress said as she brought cups and coffee to the table.

"Your sales figures must be looking good after yesterday," Mike said.

"They sure do," Sarah said "I think I need to get engaged more often."

"Once is enough for you, my dear," Andy said in as stern a voice as he could.

Mike and Andy were sitting at the end of the table.

"Got something I need to talk with you about," Andy told Mike. "We saw Harry yesterday and he asked me to come back to talk privately. So I did. He said he knows that I will be moving to Sarah's house to live. Sarah and I haven't had time to talk about that yet, but Harry thinks that anyhow. He wants me to sell his house."

Mike was quiet for a minute. "I'm not too surprised to hear that. Do you think he has completely reconciled himself to living at the care center?"

"He seems to be very content there, but I don't know him too well. It's Saturday so things should be quiet there. Would you have time to go see him? I'm not sure he really wants to let his house go, but maybe he does. I would do anything for him, but I'm just not sure about this."

"I'll go see him this afternoon," Mike said. He sat quietly among the family thinking. Then quietly, he spoke to Andy.

"Jeff and Karen will be moving to Nuna Lake. I'm not sure what kind of place they'll be looking for — something modern I would think — but maybe Harry would consider renting it if he doesn't seem like he's ready to sell. But that would, in effect, be pushing you out the door."

"I think I can find a place to hang my hat," Andy said with a smile. "But honestly, I don't know how Sarah feels. I know she looks on her house as one she grew up in. I can't imagine her wanting to live anywhere but her own house, but maybe I'm wrong. I don't know what to do."

"Let me go and talk to Harry this afternoon. I'll call you. Maybe you should tell Sarah about Harry's plans."

"I guess you're right."

That night after Sarah had closed the store, she and Andy sat quietly with their coffee.

"Are you up for a big discussion or are you too tired?" he asked.

"You sound serious. Is something wrong?"

"No, nothing's wrong. But I've been asked to do something I'm not sure about. I need your advice. You heard Harry ask me to come back out to talk with him. He also said he knows the two of us will be living at your house, so he asked me to prep his house so he can sell it. I told him I'd look into it, but I don't know what to do about it. Would it be a house you might like to live in? Harry said your house is one you must not leave. But we will have to do what's best for us. I don't think he'll have any trouble selling it, but I'm perplexed about what to do. I need your cool-headed advice."

"Wow. This is a big thing to think about. I guess I just thought we'd have two houses for a while. But if Harry thinks it's time to sell…well, what do you think?"

"Honestly, I'm not sure. I'm not even sure Harry should sell right now. Do you think he really wants to stay at the home for the rest of his life?"

"I'm not sure. I think maybe I should call Angela to see what she thinks."

"That's a good idea. I did tell Mike about it. He said he'd talk to Harry. Maybe he'll have another idea for us." Then all of a sudden he sat up straight. "I love you, Sarah. Do you have any idea how nice it is to share my problems with someone?" he said as he reached to give her a hug.

"And it is so nice to be able to talk about my shop to someone. Thanks for being so understanding about how much time I have to spend there right now."

"As long as you come home to me, I'll let you do what you want. I love you, Sarah."

"I love you, Andy."

They sat quietly for a few minutes. Then Sarah spoke.

"Harry's right, you know. I do love this house. Even when I was a young girl, I knew this house was here for me — a refuge from the world."

"Then let me move here with you. I can live anywhere, anywhere at all, if you are there Sarah. When I think back to how lonely I was in that big perfectly furnished penthouse and how lonely and desolate I felt...well, when I'm here with you I really, really feel like I have a home. I'll tell Mike tomorrow that Harry was right. I do need to move in here."

Chapter 23

The next week seemed to pass in a flurry of motion in Nuna Lake. And all of it seemed to be good. An announcement was made that the airport between Nuna Lake and Sprucedale was getting new owners. It meant there would be more jobs available. The Women's Shelter out on the highway received a big grant which would be good for both towns. The annual lighting of the Christmas Tree Celebration was very popular with people coming from many miles to take part in the celebration. And many of them came to Sarah's shop. Sales were up considerably over prior years.

Mike had talked with Harry, and Sarah talked with Angela about the sale of Harry's house. They all felt that Harry was sincere; he did want to sell his house. That made Mike a hero because Jeff and Karen, Rose's son and wife, were moving to Nuna Lake from Chicago. It would be the perfect home for them as they both were looking for a house with old-fashioned charm. They planned to move after the first of the year, and stay with Mike and Rose. Angela's sister and brother would come home from overseas to see their father and together they would go through the treasures of the past in the house. Then Jeff and Karen would move to their new home.

Things at Mike Nelson's Landscaping were quieter during the winter season. They still cleared roads and driveways in the snow. Martha, who oversaw Mike's lab work decided to retire after her surgery, and Mike asked Andy to take over the responsibility for all the lab work.

It was work Andy loved and said he'd gladly take on that responsibility.

Andy continued to live at Harry's officially but spent a lot of time at Sarah's.

They talked about being married. One day as they had coffee, Sarah said, "Andy, I've got an idea. Let's get married on New Year's Day. I'd like to start the new year as Mrs. Andrew Mellon. Maybe I'll close the shop for a week and we can get away for a few days. Would Mike be able to run the lab so you could get away?"

"It's absolutely no problem for me. But are you sure you want to have a wedding that quickly?"

"I will be starting the rest of my life. What better day than the first day of the year?"

"Yippee," he said. "I'm the luckiest man in the world."

"Let's talk to Rev. Joe to see if we can be married in the chapel at church. It's small but I have no personal family to invite and neither do you so it will be quiet and personal."

"We'll have to invite Harry, of course, Rose and Mike and their family, Julia and her family, Gabe and his family, well, I may think of a few others. Will there be room in the chapel?"

"I'm sure there will be. We can have wedding cake and punch in the reception room at the church after the service," she said.

"Where do you want to go on a honeymoon?" he asked. "We can go anywhere in the world," he told her.

"Somewhere warm and balmy," she answered. "You decide and then tell me what to pack."

"Do we plan for one or two weeks?" he asked.

"Why not two? Rose's daughter-in-law will be here to help Julia run the shop so that should not be a problem."

"And I'm sure Martha will stay on another two weeks to run the lab," and then he added "Are you sure you don't want an engagement ring?"

"I really don't think I'd be comfortable wearing it unless it was smaller than a period."

They sat quietly for a few minutes, each one with their own thoughts.

"I need a new suit," he said.

They sat quietly. Then Sarah spoke.

"Packed away in a box, I have the wedding dress worn by both my mother and her mother. It was made of lace and might be falling apart. But IF, and that's a big IF, its okay, and IF it fits, would it be okay with you if I wear it, or would it be better if I buy a new dress as we start a new life together."

"I think it would be perfect. In a way, it would be like getting their blessing. Why not get it out and try it on? Will you ask Rose or Julia to stand with you? he asked.

"Hmmm, I didn't think about that. Maybe I'll ask them both."

"Then I'll ask Mike and Gabe to stand with me."

"Then we'll be all set."

"Not so fast, lady. Not so fast. All joking aside, where to you want to go on a honeymoon? How long can you be away?" he asked.

"Let's make it two weeks."

"Somewhere warm or do you like to ski?"

"I think I'd like to put on a swim suit and sit on the sand."

"I can arrange that."

"Then surprise me."

"Any other plans we need to make?"

"I suppose so, but I'll ask Rose and Julia. They'll know."

"Sarah, I feel like I'm so happy I should sing, or maybe I should shout from the hilltops."

"Why not just come here and let me rub your back?"

"Let's go see Rev. Joe."

Rev. Joe was very happy; he said the chapel would be available. He asked if they would like to hold a small reception in the reception room or the social hall. They opted for the reception room.

"I think I'll see if Dorothy can make us a small cake. We can have that with coffee or punch. Does that sound okay? Then after a short reception we can leave on our honeymoon. I can't wait," Sarah said.

"Can you take time to do that? I know how busy you are at the shop."

"Let's go together," she said. "Maybe she can see us this morning. Julia should be okay for an hour or so."

Dorothy was very happy to be asked to cater the reception and said she'd take care of everything. She asked how many they should plan for.

223

"Let's go big," Andy said. "Maybe twenty/twenty five people. If there is anything left over we can send it to the Women's Shelter."

"Sounds good to me," Sarah said.

"I'll have some ideas ready for you tonight," she said.

Sarah called Rose and asked her and then Julia to stand with her. They were thrilled to be asked. Rose came right to the shop to coordinate with Julia. They asked Sarah what she would wear. When she mentioned the wedding dress they insisted she go home and bring it back to the shop for their approval. So she did.

It was a very simple elegant dress, no ruffles or frills: a simple floor-length sheath with a high neck and long fitted sleeves made of Alecon lace. It fit her perfectly, clinging tightly to her body. It was a quiet, dignified, extremely classy dress.

"It's perfect, just perfect," both Julia and Rose exclaimed. "But what do you want us to wear."

"Something you already have that fits you perfectly. Rose, you have that soft blue wool dress that would be perfect. And Julia, you have that rose colored dress that you look wonderful in. I really, really don't want you to go buy anything new. I don't want you coming to my wedding in twinsy dresses you'll never wear again. Please tell me you will wear the dresses you already have."

"Okay, Sarah, you're the boss." Rose said. "Are you going on a honeymoon?"

"Yes, for two weeks IF and it's a big IF, Mike gives Andy time off and dear, sweet beautiful Julia says she'll run the shop without me."

"Did you ever hear so much bull?" Julia said with a smile. "I'll have Rose, Karen, a ton of our Christmas help to stay on for a couple of weeks. We'll be fine."

As the word spread about the upcoming wedding, Rev. Joe discovered a problem. Many, many people called him to ask if they could attend. He decided to discretely ask Andy if it would present a problem. It was going to be New Year's Day and though people might plan to come, many probably would not. He called Andy to ask how to handle anyone else who might show up. Andy told him to invite them in. Then Rev. Joe called Andy again. "Do you think it would be okay to move the ceremony to the church altar instead of the chapel," he asked.

"It's not a problem," Andy told him.

Feeling a bit uncomfortable, Rev. Joe then called Dorothy and told her of his problem.

Dorothy told him not to worry; the cake would be big enough, and she would plan for 200-250 people. "But," she told him, "perhaps it would be best not to tell Sarah or Andy about it. This whole town loves Sarah and is beginning to love Andy. If they want to come and honor her I think they should. If we have food left over, I'll take it to the Women's Shelter or the Convalescent Home to honor Harry. Let's let Sarah be surprised when she sees how much the town loves her."

"I had a call from Rev. Joe today," Andy told Sarah that night. "They might move us out to the sanctuary instead of the chapel. Is that okay with you?"

"If you're there, I don't care where we are."

Sarah's shop had never had as busy and wonderful Christmas season. She was happy that she sold almost all of her Christmas stock and was especially pleased when they saw how many other pieces of regular merchandise she sold. The "Wells for Africa" project had done extremely well. They sold every one of the hundred crèches she had for sale and their contributions were very generous. She wrote a check for $5000 to send for the project.

Andy slowly moved his personal belongings out of Harry's and into Sarah's house. The house would be sold to Jeff and Karen.

Andy did finally buy a suit. It almost felt strange to him because he hadn't worn a suit for months. People in Nuna Lake dressed very casual. He also shopped for a wedding ring. One day he had a passing thought about his first wedding. There were 400 people invited. He was constantly being told what to do or where to go. He had no part in the planning. But as he thought about that marriage, it was the same way. Someone was always telling him what to do or where to go. He wondered why he let people push him around so. It wouldn't happen today. But then, it wasn't even anything he had to think about. He'd do somersaults down the aisle if Sarah asked him. He loved her so.

Sarah couldn't believe she was really getting married. After her long-time romance with the jerk, he made her feel like she was unworthy of being loved. But Andy made her feel so special, like he couldn't live without her. She loved him so.

Christmas came and went as almost an afterthought to the upcoming wedding. Sarah's shop was filled with customers each day. Sales had never been so high. Sarah planned to close the shop at 4 o'clock New Year's Eve. Their wedding was set for 2:30 p.m. on New Year's Day. The guests would then be home early and Sarah and Andy would be on their way for a honeymoon.

Their plans seemed so simple, so casual. Andy hadn't told her where he was taking her on her honeymoon. But he did tell her to pack her swimsuit so she guessed it was somewhere warm. He also asked her if it was okay to fly commercial instead of using his personal plane. She started to laugh and told him she had only been in a personal plane twice, going and coming from Arizona when they got Harry. Andy said he didn't want to spoil family holiday time for Joe and Hank.

Sarah got a bit misty-eyed when she thought about Harry. Somehow, deep in her mind, she always imagined he would walk her down the aisle. But she told him she would come to see him as soon as she was married to receive his blessing. He really had been a father-figure for most of her life.

Rose and Julia came to Sarah's house to help her dress for her wedding. Her hairdresser had come to the house early that morning to style her hair and do her nails, so Sarah was feeling pampered when they arrived. When she put on her dress, she was radiant.

"I never thought I'd ever get married," she told them. "I was prepared to spend my life alone. But now I can't imagine not having Andy in my life. And there are two things I'm sure of: I love Andy and I know he loves me."

Since the church was fairly close to her house, she waited until three o'clock to be driven to the church. Tim, Mike's son came to drive her there. "She is sort of like my big sister," he told the family. She was shocked when she saw so many cars in the parking lot at the church.

"Someone's probably having a party nearby and parking there," he told Sarah.

She went in the side door right to the bridal room where she met Rose and Julia. They wore the dresses Sarah had asked them to wear, Rose in the in the soft blue and Julia in the rose. They carried small nosegays of flowers that Gabe had flown in from Chicago.

After what seemed like hours of waiting, they made their way to the back of the sanctuary for the walk down the aisle.

Sarah could not believe her eyes at the scene. The church was beautiful. Nosegays with white ribbons decorated the ends of each pew. Gabe handed Sarah a bouquet of white flowers to carry down the aisle.

She stood there. Through the windows in the back of the sanctuary she saw the altar was draped in white with flowers everywhere. But she was shocked! Every pew was filled with people. They had invited no one but everyone wanted to honor Sarah. She turned to Rose and Julia who just smiled and said everyone asked to be part of the celebration.

"I can't believe it. I can't believe it," she kept saying.

"There's another surprise for you," Rose said as the doors behind them opened.

In the doors came Tim pushing a wheelchair and in the chair sat Harry.

"I came to walk you down the aisle," he said. "You're my other daughter."

"Oh, oh." She started to cry.

"Don't start crying," Julia said. "You'll ruin your make-up"

"I can't believe this. I can't believe this." Sarah kept saying.

Harry started to laugh. "I did fool you. I said I couldn't be here. But Tim is going to follow us down the aisle with my chair in case I start to fall. But I don't think I need him."

"I still can't believe all this," Sarah repeated. "I don't know whether to laugh or cry."

"Laugh, laugh, laugh," Harry said. "This is a happy day. I love you, Sarah, my child."

Julia and Rose had already gone down the aisle.

Harry stood, took Sarah's arm and started her down the aisle.

Tim followed discretely with the wheel chair.

When they reached the altar, Harry sat back down in the wheel chair and Tim moved him to the end of a pew.

When Sarah looked to the front as she approached the altar, she saw Andy standing there, tall and handsome; waiting for her. She was moved to tears. She had never felt so special in her life. She had never felt so loved.

When Andy saw Sarah approaching the altar on the arm of Harry, he thought he had never been so happy in his life. He loved her so much. He saw the crowd of people gathered in that place to honor Sarah. He couldn't believe this outpouring of love from the town for them. He then realized that he was no longer an outsider in town, they had come to honor him as well.

Quietly and somberly they pledged their vows to each other. When Rev. Joe asked for the rings, Sarah handed him a solid gold band. Andy presented a gold wedding ring with diamonds across the top for Sarah. It was quietly elegant.

When the minister pronounced them man and wife, everyone started to clap for them.

"My life is just now beginning," Andy said quietly to Sarah.

"My life is just now beginning," Sarah answered quietly.

Then they turned to their guests amidst cheering and clapping.

Chapter 24

"Andy, can you believe this," Sarah asked as the bridal party walked to the Social Room of the church.

"Nope," he said with a smile. "But you deserve it. You are so loved in this town."

"Now do you believe how much this town loves you," Rose asked as they made their way.

"Did you know all this was going on?" Sarah asked Rose.

"Actually, Dorothy called to let me know she was catering the event and for you not to worry about anything. I told her I knew you were so busy and expected to have less than twenty people there. She just laughed at me and told me not to worry. So I didn't. But this is wonderful. You have done so much for this town, always being there with a kind word. I think every kid in high school has worked for you one time or another. They all wanted to be here," Rose added.

"Well, I am shocked by it all. But this is truly the happiest day of my life."

"Gabe is responsible for all the flowers. Remember, he did the same for me when Mike and I were married," Rose told her.

The Social Room had been transformed into a garden with flowers and greenery everywhere. A special archway had been placed so Sarah and Andy could stand there and receive guests. They gradually were pushed into place. There was no formal receiving line yet there were always four or five people there to greet the couple.

"Congratulations, Andy." Andy was surprised to see his good friends, Hank and Joe greeting him along with their wives.

"How did you know?" he asked them.

"Your business manager told us. We thought that we should be here. I called Mike and he said it was okay as this was a casual affair. Anyhow, it gave our wives a chance to see Nuna Lake since we'll be moving here. Do you have arrangements made to leave town on your honeymoon or can we take you somewhere?"

"I didn't want to bother you on the holidays so I booked us commercial."

"Want to change your plans?"

"No, you stay here and meet everyone in town. The mayor is over there," Andy said pointing to his left. "Go and introduce yourselves. I've told him all about you. He is anxious to meet you."

Andy looked up to greet the next in line. He broke into a smile and said, "I don't believe it." Standing there was his good friend, Dr. David Hass and his wife.

"How did you know…how did you get here…I can't believe it." Andy stuttered for words.

"You're buying me a new piece of equipment, remember. I called your business manager and he told me you were getting married today. So I invited myself and my wife. And…"

"But how did you get here to Nuna Lake?" Andy interrupted.

"Do you think you're the only one that has a plane? Anyhow, I wanted to see Hobie. We brought someone with us." He turned to the persons behind him. "I think you know these people."

Andy looked and could not believe it! It was Mima and Lauren. "I don't believe this," he said as he reached out to give Mima a big hug. Then he turned to Sarah.

"Sarah, this is Mima. Mima, this is Sarah."

Sarah immediately gave Mima a big hug. "I am so, so glad to meet you. Andy has told me so much about you – how you took care of him – how…"

Mima interrupted Sarah. "I think I kept him safe so he could find you. When he told me he loved you I saw the love in his eyes and the love in his heart. You are married to a fine man. I'm so happy to have the chance to know you."

"How did this all happen?" Andy asked David.

"When I called about the equipment (which you told me to do) your business manager told me you were being married today. I knew Mima had come to visit Lauren and thought it would be a nice surprise to bring them to your wedding. I had Mike Nelson's name on file so I called him to ask if it would be okay. He said it was."

"It's more than okay, it's wonderful."

"No," Mima said. "What's wonderful is that you have found a good woman. I knew you would find her. Getting to meet you is a wonderful event for me," she said to Sarah.

"Mima, your being here is like having a family here. I'm so glad to see you."

"Well, I'll send you a bill for the gasoline," David said with a smile.

"I still can't believe it," Andy said. "You have made this day perfect."

Mike had been standing nearby. He came up to David and said, "I think you said you'd like to like to see Hobie. I'll take you to him. He's right over here."

"Can you believe it?" Andy asked Sarah.

"I don't think I can believe this day. It has been perfect, just perfect."

"It might be getting time for us to leave for the airport. I think we should get ready to go."

"And where are we going?" she asked.

"To the Nuna Lake airport so we can get to Chicago."

"Ah, a honeymoon in Chicago. I think I've been there once or twice."

"Well, maybe we won't stay in Chicago. Maybe we'll spend the night at the airport hotel and get on another plane tomorrow."

"And where might that plane take us," she asked.

"California."

"Wonderful."

"But we won't stay there."

"No, hmmm, I wonder where we'll go next."

"How about Tahiti? Would that be too boring?"

"Tahiti?" Sarah shouted. "I'm going to Tahiti!"

Those people closest to her began to gather around her.

"Oh, Andy, I do love you. I'll always try to make you happy," Sarah said as she gave him a big hug.

"You have already done that" he answered.

Andy then walked to the podium placed in the room and asked for everyone's attention. "Thank you to each one of you who came here today. I came to town because I heard Nuna Lake was a nice place to live. Nuna Lake is beautiful. But it is the people who make it wonderful. Today, Sarah and I expected to see a handful of people. To see so many of you here….well, it was a big surprise. I know Sarah deserves your tribute. She's so wonderful. But you also welcomed me, a stranger, into your town. I thank you for that. Sarah, do you want to say anything."

"Yes, I do. I can only add my thanks to what Andy said. But as I look at you all, I realize you all are my family. I think I could call everyone of you by name. I know I thought I wanted a small, private wedding ceremony. It may not have been private, but this is a gathering of the very special people who are the real Nuna Lake. Thank you for sharing this beautiful day with us. You are all my family. I love you all."

Gabe came up to them. "I think you'd better change so we can get to the airport. You don't want to miss your plane."

"Did Andy tell you where we're going?" Sarah asked Gabe.

"I think I heard you shouting, Tahiti."

"She said she wants to sit in the warm sand," Andy told Gabe.

"This whole wedding is for two special people. The town is glad you two got married, they are glad you let them be a part of it. But now it's time for just the two of you. Hurry off and have a great honeymoon, but don't forget you both really belong to Nuna Lake. We want you, we need you, we love you."

Printed in the United States
By Bookmasters